BEAUTY FOUND

A Hades Hangmen Novella

Tillie Cole

BEAUTY FOUND

Copyright© Tillie Cole 2018 All rights reserved

Copyedited by www.kiathomasediting.com
Formatted by Stephen Jones
Cover Design by Damonza.com

Paperback Copy

No Part of this publication may be reproduced or transmitted in any form or by any means, electronic or mechanical, including photography, recording, or any information storage and retrieval system without the prior written consent from the publisher and author, except in the instance of quotes for reviews. No part of this book may be uploaded without the permission of the publisher and author, nor be otherwise circulated in any form of binding or cover other than that in which it is originally published.

This is a work of fiction and any resemblance to persons, living or dead, or places, actual events or locales is purely coincidental. The characters and names are products of the author's imagination and used fictitiously.

The publisher and author acknowledge the trademark status and trademark ownership of all trademarks, service marks and word marks mentioned in this book.

Hades Hangmen Terminology

Hades Hangmen: *One-percenter Outlaw MC. Founded in Austin, Texas, 1969.*

Hades: *Lord of the Underworld in Greek mythology.*

Mother Chapter: *First branch of the club. Founding location.*

One-percenter: *The American Motorbike Association (AMA) were once rumored to have said that 99% of bikers were law-abiding citizens. Bikers who do not abide by AMA rules name themselves 'one-percenters' (the remaining non law-abiding 1%). The vast majority of 'one-percenters' belong to Outlaw MC's.*

Cut: *Leather vest worn by outlaw bikers. Adorned with patches and artwork displaying the club's unique colors.*

Patched in: *When a new member is approved for full membership.*

Church: *Club meetings for full patch members. Led by President of the club.*

Old Lady: *Woman with wife status. Protected by her partner. Status held to be sacrosanct by club members.*

Club Slut: *A woman who comes to the clubhouse to engage in casual sexual acts with the club members.*

Bitch: *Woman in Biker culture. Term of endearment*

Gone/Going to Hades: *Slang. Referring to the dying/dead.*

Meeting/Gone/Going to the Boatman: *Slang. Dying/dead. Referring to 'Charon' in Greek mythology. Charon was the ferryman of the dead, an underworld daimon (Spirit). Transported departed souls to Hades. The fee for the crossing over the rivers Styx and Acheron to Hades were coins placed on either the dead's eyes or mouth at burial. Those who did not pay the fee were left to wander the shores of Styx for one hundred years.*

Snow: *Cocaine.*

Ice: *Crystal Meth.*

Smack: *Heroin*

The Organizational Structure of Hades Hangmen

President (Prez): *Leader of the club. Holder of the Gavel, which is symbolic of the absolute power that the President wields. The Gavel is used to keep order in Church. The word of* *the President is law within the club. He takes advice from senior club members. No one challenges the decisions of the President.*

Vice President (VP): *Second-in-Command. Executes the orders of the President. Principal communicator with other chapters of the club. Assumes all responsibilities and duties of the President in his absence.*

Road Captain: *Responsible for all club runs. Researches, plans and organizes club runs and ride outs. Ranking club officer, answering only to President or VP.*

Sergeant-at-Arms: *Responsible for club security, policing and keeping order at club events. Reports unseemly behavior to President and VP. Responsible for the safety and protection of the club, its members and its Prospects.*

Treasurer: *Keeps records of all income and expenses. Keeps records of all club patches and colors issued and taken away.*

Secretary: *Responsible for making and keeping all club records. Must notify members of emergency meetings.*

Prospect: *Probationary member of the MC. Goes on runs, but banned from attending Church.*

Dedication

To the Hangmen Harem.

You asked for their story.

Here it is.

PROLOGUE

Tank

Age 17

I wasn't even awake when the first boot hit my ribs. I gasped, my eyes shooting open as another boot smashed into my stomach, knocking the wind right out of me. I scrambled back against the wall and looked up. There were at least five of them that I could see. A fist plowed into my face as I tried to get up, knocking me the fuck back down. "Asshole!" I hissed, and pushed back at the prick who was trying to keep me on the ground. He slammed to the floor. I jumped up just in time to see one of the fuckers grab my backpack.

"Hey!" I barked. But before I could rush at him, charge the bastard for touching my things, four others flew at me. Fists and feet pounded into my body. Black dots started dancing in my eyes, then suddenly the assholes were ripped away.

I leaned against the wall, holding my ribs, catching my fucking breath, and looked up. A group of tatted-up white guys were smashing their fists into a bunch of Mexicans . . . the fuckers that had attacked me.

It was a quick fight, the new guys kicking the asses of the Mexicans in minutes. The fuckers ran away down the alley in which I'd been sleeping. Sweat and blood dripped down my face. As I wiped it away with my hand, my vision cleared to see a huge guy with a shaved head approaching, my backpack in his hands.

"They didn't get anything?" he said. I narrowed my eyes. He had a massive skull and crossbones in the middle of his throat. I reached out and took hold of my backpack. My teeth gritted together at the immediate stab of pain in my ribs.

The fuckers had broken them. I just knew it.

The guy pulled the bag back and grabbed my arm. His hand was like a vise around my bicep. He smirked. "How old are you, kid?"

I cast my eyes around the others. They all looked the same—same haircut, clothes, tattoos. And they were all looking at me. "About to be eighteen."

The guy shook his head. "You're a big fucker." I shucked off his arm and stepped back, ignoring the pain in my ribs. It wasn't like I'd never coped with this shit before. "Football?"

"Tight end," I said after a few moments of saying fuck all. "Varsity . . . at least I was."

The guy looked at someone behind him, then back at me. "And now you're sleeping in an alley?"

Every muscle in me tensed. This asshole had no fucking idea of the shit I'd been through. I couldn't have stayed with my old man for another damn minute. My jaw clenched and my hand rolled into a fist at my side. Sudden anger lit me the fuck up as I thought of him taking one of his fists to my face after he got jacked up on whiskey . . . again. The guy must have seen it. But instead of being threatened, he just smiled wider and whispered something to the guy behind him again. He stepped closer, his height and build matching mine. "I'm Trace."

I looked around at them all. None of them seemed like they wanted to kill me, and they'd kicked those Mexicans' asses for me too. "Shane. Shane Rutherford."

Trace smiled. "Good name. Pure. True American." He pointed to my ribs. "We got someone who can fix that."

My eyes narrowed. "Why would you do that?" I tensed. "I ain't sucking your dick." I'd had too many of those offers here on the streets.

Trace burst out laughing, as did the rest of the guys behind him. "Good to know. Like fags 'bout as much as I like Mexicans."

My shoulders lost their tension, but I still asked, "Why're you helping me?"

Trace put his arm around my shoulder and turned so I could see all the guys with him. "When a white brother, from good American stock, US of A born and bred, is in need, his fellow white brothers come to help."

The tattoos on the guys' arms and necks became clear. Swastikas, Celtic crosses, "SS." "We got a place you can stay. We can fix you with a job, get you outta this alley." I glanced back at the blanket I'd been sleeping on for two months. My stomach growled in hunger. Trace squeezed my shoulder. "Food you can eat."

"Johnny Landry makes insane barbeque," one of the other guys said. Barbeque was my fucking favorite.

They all stared at me. Trace kept hold of my shoulder. I sighed, for the first time in weeks feeling something but fucking desperate. "I could eat some barbeque," I said, and the guys smiled.

"Then let's get the fuck on." Trace led me to a truck. I took a deep breath as we left downtown Austin and continued out toward Spicewood. We turned and drove down a dirt road until a house came into view. Dozens of people sat outside, drinking and talking.

"The brotherhood," Trace said. I looked at him. He must have been about twenty-four, twenty-five? Trace took me into the house. A group of guys were in the massive kitchen. They looked different to Trace and his friends. They looked smarter in their fancier clothes. Spoke different. Sounded like they did more than fight gangs on the street.

An older guy with suspicious eyes got to his feet. "Who's this?" he asked as he flicked his chin.

"Shane Rutherford," Trace said. "Found him getting mugged by spics. Couldn't leave a brother to get beaten down that way."

The older guy nodded. "Jay's in the back room. He'll fix him up." I followed Trace down a hallway to a back room. The place was mostly wood paneled,

American and Nazi flags pinned on most of the walls. Then, at the end, was a huge fuck-off painting of Hitler.

Motherfucking Adolf Hitler.

I stopped dead, just staring at that picture. I wasn't stupid. In fact, I'd been pretty fucking smart throughout school. Good with mechanics. Engineering, that kind of shit. And I'd paid attention in European History class. I was fully fucking aware of Hitler. Knew some about white power and the KKK. Never given them much thought. They'd never been part of my life. But as Hitler's fierce eyes bored into mine from the painting, some kind of new pounding settled in my chest.

Laughter came from down the hallway. A window sat to the right of me, and I looked out at the men in the yard. They were drinking American beer and

Scottish fucking whiskey and having the time of their lives. My gut pulled as I realized I'd never really had a group of friends like that. I'd had football. But when your old man was an alcoholic whose favorite hobby was smashing his fist into his son's face, it made you close in. None of those guys knew what it was to be me. I'd played football because I was a huge fucker who needed to hit people. To get out this rage. My old man was even bigger than me. No matter how much I fought back, that bastard always won.

One of the guys turned up the volume on a stereo, and some rock song blared from the speaker. He screamed the lyrics. About brotherhood and being a white American. I felt the beats from the song travel through my veins like crack.

I wanted to be out there with them. Fucking drinking and not giving a shit about anything but the men around me.

"You good?" Trace spoke from behind me. I turned and gave him a nod. He took hold of my arm and pulled me into a smaller room off the hallway. A tall, thin guy with brown hair stood beside a bed made up with white sheets.

The guy held out his hand. "Jay." I introduced myself.

"Ex-Army," Trace said, pointing at Jay. "Medic." Trace slapped Jay on the back. "Served for this fucking country. Taking down cunts that try to take away our freedom." Trace smiled. "Fucking white hero."

"Thank you for your service."

Jay nodded, and I could tell by the glint in his eyes that I'd just done something right. "Sit on the bed." Jay sent Trace away, then stitched up my cuts and strapped up my ribs. The whole time he told me about how he'd had a similar background to me. Found his home here with Johnny Landry. Then he joined the army. Wanted to fight for his country. Told me most of the brothers at this ranch did. They were American soldiers, not thugs. Landry had a bigger mission than just street fights with Mexicans and blacks. With every word spoken, my heart beat faster and faster, hanging off everything he said. Family . . . brothers . . . a cause . . . a reason for living . . . Those words lit me up like the fourth of July.

When he was done, Jay put his hand on my shoulder. "You need to talk to Landry, kid. You're the kind of solider he's looking for. I can tell." He tapped his head. "You got something up here"—he laughed—"As well as all that fucking muscle." Then he left, leaving me alone.

I couldn't get his words from my head. I was what Landry was looking for. A smirk pulled at the corner of my mouth.

I knocked back the pain meds Jay had handed me along with the can of beer he'd given me to take them with.

I ran my hand down my face, suddenly dead tired, but my mind racing with what had happened. With that picture of Hitler looking at me like he could see through me. With Landry's eyes staring at me as I'd walked in. When I opened my eyes, someone was in the doorway. The guy looked my age, maybe a bit younger. My gaze narrowed on him.

"Trace said the spics got you."

"Tried," I said after a few seconds of silence. "Your boys chased them off."

"You play football." It wasn't a question. "Trace said." Looked like Trace had given everyone the rundown while Jay had been fixing me up.

"Tight end," I said. "In high school. Just left. Graduated early, then got the fuck out."

The guy nodded. "I'm a quarterback." He stepped further into the room. He had no tattoos. But the kid was built and tall too. "A freshman." He seemed more upmarket than me and the others here. Spoke better than Trace. Sure spoke better than my redneck ass. Didn't seem like the rest of the folks here. And the kid sure as shit didn't look like a freshman.

"I'm Tanner." He put his hand out for me to shake.

Holding my ribs with one hand, I gave him my other. "Shane."

"Tank, more like," Trace said from behind Tanner. "You haven't eaten in weeks yet you're still that big? Fuck Shane—you're Tank to us now."

"And who *is* us?" I asked, my eyes going from Tanner to Trace. I knew they were white power or some shit. But I had no idea just who they were.

"Your new family." Trace hooked his arm around Tanner's shoulders, pulling him close like he'd done to me. "Brothers, Tank. Fucking brothers-in-arms."

CHAPTER ONE

Tank

Five years later...

I grabbed the bag holding my stuff and moved to the back of the room to get dressed. The prison uniform fell to the floor, and I slipped on my jeans, shirt, and leather jacket—all of which were now too tight. Years of lifting weights in prison would do that to a guy.

"Sign here and here," the guard instructed. After two signatures and a long walk down a hallway, I came to the door that promised my freedom. I rocked from side to side, my hands clenching. Because walking outta this fucking door after what Landry had ordered meant I was probably walking out only to get a bullet in my skull. I touched the scar on my head. The ridges were still rough and the fucker still stung.

Only the fact that I was a hard bastard who most didn't dare fuck with had kept me from leaving this shithole in a wooden box.

The door creaked open, and I stepped out into the world.

Three years. Three years without freedom. Should have been a fuck-ton more, but all of us who went down that day knew we'd only be in there a few years max. Had to play the game so our Wizards could stay under the radar.

We should've all been serving twenty-five to life. But here I was, out in the fucking burning Texas sun after three years.

My boots crunched on the gravel as I made my way to the outer gate. The guard waited at his post, ready to release me back into the wild. My heart beat faster with every step. My hands curled into fists as I prepped for whatever would meet me on the other side of that iron. The brotherhood that had saved me and given me a life was no doubt about to take it away.

The bolt of the gate clanged, the handle turned, and the Texas heat smashed over my face to greet me. I stepped out of the gate, breath held for the gunshot, the knife, whatever the fuck it was that was waiting.

But I stopped dead when I saw a familiar truck parked up on the side of the road. My breath came out real fucking stuttered when I saw my best friend waiting beside it, arms crossed over his chest.

Tanner. Tanner fucking Ayers was the one who would be taking me out. I'd assumed he was still on tour. Was he back just for this?

I walked across the road. All the time Tanner didn't move. His eyes were on me, right up until I stopped a few feet away. The only time they moved was to glance at the shank scar on my head. He was my best friend. My brother. My fucking family. But Tanner Ayers was the White Prince, the knight of the Ku Klux fucking Klan.

And, to him, I was a traitor.

"Didn't expect you." My voice sounded as though I'd swallowed a ton of gravel.

Tanner moved around the truck and got in without a word. I took a deep breath in then got in the passenger side. Tanner burned rubber away from the prison, leaving dust in our wake. White-power rock spewed from the sound system, talking about fucking over anyone who wasn't white.

Tanner drove faster and faster until the prison was a dot in the background. He turned left down a deserted dirt road, then screeched his truck to a stop, turning the radio off. We skidded a few yards before the truck stopped and the cabin was filled with nothing but thick silence.

I kept my eyes straight forward. Didn't wanna see the face of my best friend as he took me out. The minute hand of the clock on the dashboard ticked by five times before he quietly asked, "Is it true?" My jaw clenched as his words hit my ears. When I didn't answer, Tanner slammed his hand on the steering wheel and spat, "Is it fucking true?"

I stared hard at the dying tree at the side of the barren dirt road. The branches, dry and cracked, slowly falling to the ground. "Yes," I said through gritted teeth. My gaze fell to my hands . . . to the fucking white-pride tattoo that stared back. The St. George shield that took up most of my right arm.

Tanner said fuck all after that. It was a few minutes before I looked over at him. His face was blank, staring through the windshield.

"You're my fucking brother, Tank." His voice was quiet, raw as all hell. His head finally turned to me. Brother was still without tattoos. He was in the army, doing his American duty. In communications or some shit. Tanner was never just gonna be on the front line, shooting at whichever fucker threatened our lands. They'd seen he was a fucking genius and put that brain of his to work. Of course, all that communications shit would only benefit the Klan. The heir knowing how to hack computers? A fucking gift in Landry's hands.

Tanner was nothing like the kid I'd met that day years ago on the Spicewood land. Tanner Ayers was finally the white prince his family had groomed him to be. Savage, smart as fuck, and didn't bat an eye about slitting an enemy fucker's throat.

That now included mine.

"You fucked up. Landry expected you to be with him on that kill." He shook his head, and a flush of rage climbed up his neck. "He fucking counted on his second in command in that place, and you bailed!" His breath was coming quick now. "Why? Why the fuck do you care about a fucking nothing spic?" He looked at me like he didn't know me. Like we hadn't shed blood side by side for the cause.

But that spic he spoke of, he weren't *nothing*. I'd gotten to know him. Shared a room with him for a while before Landry pulled some strings and got me with a fellow Aryan brother. I thought back to the day I'd met him . . .

The minute he entered the cell, I smashed his back against the wall. "You listen to me, you fucking dirty spic. You even breathe wrong in my direction and I'll slit your throat and let you choke on your own blood."

The spic met my eyes, then fucking laughed. "Sure you will."

My hands fisted his shirt as rage surged through me. I shoved him back, then spat, "I ain't going back into solitary again, so just stay the fuck outta my way and don't make me kill you."

The kid, because no way was he older than eighteen, pushed past me and lay on his bed. "Chill the fuck out. I don't intend on getting in anyone's way." He moved to the bed and picked up a book. He looked at me over the pages. "This is a book. You should read one." He paused. "And not the shit that's been doctored for your 'people.'" He waved it in my face. "Real books. By real people with real problems. Ideas about how to resolve those problems . . . no matter what their skin color or religion." My lip curled as he turned and started reading. Landry would get me to another cell. I just had to try not to kill this prick before that happened.

Turned out Carlos was a good kid. But a kid that had fucked up and made an enemy of the wrong guy—Johnny Landry. Hadn't known to keep his mouth shut, spouting from his books and making us KKK brothers look like idiots. Landry was just out of isolation when it all went down. I got the message, but I took as much damn time as I could getting there. I knew I couldn't save Carlos if Landry wanted him dead, but I knew I couldn't help kill him either. Turned up to see Carlos bleeding out on the floor, that fucking book he loved so much on the floor beside him, the shiv I'd given him sticking out of Brant's neck—one of our soldiers, fucking dead too.

Staring down at the pool of blood, at his eyes frozen over with death, something in me cracked. The kid was just a mouthy kid. But to Landry, he was standing in the way of making us a pure race. He'd had to be taken out. Carlos's mouth had had to be shut for good. I'd warned the kid. But he hadn't listened.

I stopped eating with them all after that. Kept the fuck away when Carlos's dead eyes would never leave my head.

And in turn, I signed my own death sentence.

"I want out." I met Tanner's furious eyes. "Want the fuck out of this life."

"The war's coming," he said slowly, like I was a dumbfuck. "The race war is fucking coming."

I laughed. Fucking laughed. "There ain't no race war, Tann. It's all bullshit." I'd read some of Carlos's books. In prison, I wasn't the trailer-park kid that owed the Klan my fealty, blindly following them into shootouts and murders. I finally used my fucking brain for the first time in five years, and I realized it was all a crock of shit. Tanner's cheek twitched in annoyance. "You're the fucking smartest person I've ever known. You know it's all bullshit; you have to. Wake the fuck up!"

Tanner shook his head, like he was going to argue. But he didn't. He couldn't. Because he knew I was right. We'd been fed racist shit until our veins ran with the white and red of the Klan. Mexicans and blacks and Jews and gays were nothing, rats to be taken down. A pollution to the world and the white race that reigned supreme. I lived it, breathed it, drank the fucking Kool-Aid, and killed and beat and spat on anyone that wasn't like us.

I'd fought in the street beside Landry, our leader, until a black guy was dead. My sentence for my part—five years. Out in three for "good behavior." In truth, it was because we had an influential Wizard on our side—the most influential in Texas, fuck, in the USA. Landry wouldn't be far behind me. He would never have been locked up in the first place, but a black cop arrested us, the case was made into news, and we'd had to play the game. No one was allowed to know who Landry's big brother was.

Whose Tanner's old man really was.

"We're going to a ranch rally." Tanner pulled back out onto the road. The radio came on. The music pounded, seeming like it was getting louder with every mile we got closer to the Spicewood ranch.

It would go down there.

End where it all began.

"Just know I fucking love you like a brother," I said over the music. I wasn't even sure Tanner had heard me. "Still do. Nothing will change that. Klan or no Klan. You're my fucking brother."

From the day I'd arrived at the ranch, Tanner had been there. From that day on, he'd stuck with me. We were young compared to a lot of the others. It made sense that we'd become close. Didn't know I was aligning myself with the White Prince. Didn't know that friendship would take me into the inner circle of the Austin KKK. A true brother, one who was valuable.

One whose only ticket out was death.

Tanner didn't respond to what I'd said. He never said shit as we crossed the city limits of Austin, nor as we rolled down the track of the Spicewood KKK ranch, where I could hear music and see fire licking at wooden crosses.

The minute the truck pulled to a stop, all eyes were on us. Tanner's hands were iron grips on the wheel. Then, "I'm gonna fucking miss you, asshole." Tanner got out of the truck, and I knew I had minutes left.

It was a strange feeling, knowing you were about to die by the hands of the people who'd once saved your life. But what surprised me most was the calm in my veins. I supposed I'd always thought I'd end up dying for this Klan. Just never thought it'd be as a deserter.

Tanner opened the passenger-side door, took my arm, and wrenched me from the truck. My brothers stormed forward, some still in their hoods from the rally. Tanner's hand gripped the back of my neck. "Fucking knew he wasn't a turncoat," Tanner said. *What the . . . ?* He didn't give me time to show my shock, as he continued, "Brant, the asshole, wanted up Landry's ass. He never passed on the message to our boy Tank here and lied to my uncle. Only to die killing a weak-as-piss spic. That's why Tank was late. He got the message too late." He spat on the floor, then his hand went to my scar. "Tank got shanked because of the cunt, but he still managed to fight Aaron, who did it, off, staying alive to fight the upcoming war!" Brothers nodded their heads, and I saw the pride in their eyes. "I'll get word to Landry that one of our best white soldiers is free and more dedicated to the cause than ever!"

Cheers went up around the Klansmen, and I was bombarded with drinks and hugs and "welcome homes." I stepped back to see Tanner grab a bottle of whiskey and walk to the side of the property.

A hard hand landed on my back. "Knew it." I looked up to see Beau Ayers, Tanner's younger brother. I would recognize his graveled voice anywhere. "You're no traitor." Beau looked back at his big brother. They looked nothing alike. Beau had longish brown hair and brown eyes. And Beau Ayers was a damn fortress. Kept to himself. Had no one around him except his brother. And me on occasion.

Right now was the most I'd ever heard the brother speak since we'd met. "He wasn't the same without you. He's only on leave from the army for a few more weeks. The minute he heard what happened, he told everyone he could that it was bullshit. That he'd bet his life there was some mistake." Beau rocked awkwardly on his feet, crossing his bulking arms over his chest. "My brother's always right."

Guilt cut through me, thick and fast. Tanner had trusted me. Defended me.

Beau walked away, disappearing into the ranch house, keeping the fuck away from everyone else. I scanned around for Tanner, but there was no sign of him. The liquor flowed; the "welcome homes" flowed too.

An arm hooked around my neck. "Tank!" Calvin Roberts's drunken voice hit my ears. I looked up to see a crowd of my brothers gathering around me. Calvin held up his bottle of liquor to get everyone's attention. "Tell us what went down that day. When you fucking ended Keon Walters and his crew. We've all heard the stories. Jerked off to the description of the fucking kills. But we wanna hear it from your mouth. One of the real fucking heroes."

Keon Walters. That name pierced through my skull. *Keon . . . Keon . . . Keon . . .* His face flashed before my eyes. His battered face. The feel of his shoulders under my hand, and the smell of his blood as it pooled on the floor . . .

"What?" Landry answered his cell. We were driving back from making a deal with the Aryan Brotherhood. More allies for the war that was coming. Landry hung up without saying anything else. But his face had frosted over to fucking ice, and he jerked on the steering wheel, suddenly heading right. His foot was lead on the gas.

"What's going on?" I asked, my heart starting to pound knowing something was big was going down.

"Keon and his crew are out near Marble Falls. Cutting some deal on our fucking soil." Landry was so filled with rage that he spat when he spoke. I felt the familiar heat of hate travel

through my veins, lighting me the fuck up inside. My leg bounced, itching for the fight I knew was coming.

"Brant just called it in. They're there now, waiting for us." Nodding, I reached into my jeans and pulled out my knife and gun. My shoulders tensed, my eyes scanning around us as Landry pushed his truck to its fastest speed.

Keon Walters was a piece of shit. Trying to come onto our soil and trade guns out from under us. I glanced at Landry. His face was beet red. Keon Walters had fucked up three months ago when he'd taken out Landry's childhood best friend. Roy Harris had been shot through the head.

Keon Walters had held the gun.

Landry had been waiting for this day.

"Five of them," Landry said, clearly referring to how many of Keon's men were making the deal. "The black bastard is there too." Landry smiled. It was the coldest fucking smile I'd ever seen.

My heart beat faster, excitement at the thought of Keon dying a slow and painful death under our white hands making my dick hard. I gripped my knife tighter, putting my gun into the waistband of my jeans. A minute later, I jumped out of the truck into fucking chaos. Brant and Charles were charging across the back street, guns firing back at Keon's crew, who were taking cover behind dumpsters. A slug made its hit on Charles, and his body slumped to the floor.

I glanced down, seeing his eyes wide open and a bullet wound in his head. My hands gripped the knife so tight I almost broke the fucking handle. "Cunt!" I snarled and started running across the street. I made it to the first fucker before he'd even had the chance to run. I stabbed the knife into his tattooed neck and watched him drop to the ground, his crew's colored bandana dropping beside him.

I moved to the next asshole, taking my gun from my jeans and sending a bullet straight into the impure fucker's heart. I smiled, a cold damn smile, as his eyes locked on me and blood dripped from his mouth. The last thing he'd ever see was a Klan brother, smiling at him as he drained of life.

"Tank!" I snapped my head to the back of the far-off dumpster. Landry was fighting to keep one of the bastards in his grip. The closer I ran, the faster my pulse raced. Keon Walters. Brant appeared beside me—cut up, injured, but fighting on. He'd taken out a couple of these pricks too.

Landry threw Keon into me. I didn't waste time; I smashed my fist into the fucker's face and pummeled him into the ground. It was only Landry dragging me away that stopped me from ending the fucker right then.

"Hold him down!" Landry ordered. I put my rage aside and did as he said, pushing down on Keon's shoulders. Landry got above him and smiled that fucking cold smile again. He brought his knife to Keon's face. Keon tried to break from my

hands, but I was too strong. The asshole couldn't even move an inch.

The sound of police sirens blared in the distance.

"Landry," I warned. "We need to get out of here. Now."
This place was too public. Someone had seen us. Not all the cops were on our payroll.

His eyes narrowed on me. "I won't rush this." He brought his knife to Keon's throat and slowly sliced across his skin. Just to watch him bleed. "This is worth doing time for." He met my eyes. "If we're arrested by one who isn't ours, we'll only be in for a few years. You know we have protection against anything more. It's our duty to get this revenge. This is for the Klan, Tank. For the brotherhood. For Roy..." He focused on Keon. "Now. Hold the impure bastard down. I'm gonna make this fucker scream..."

The sound of a truck backfiring cut through the memory and brought me back to the here and now.

Calvin's arm slipped from me, and he and his brothers went toward the sound of the noise. Some new drunk asshole drag racing on the land, no doubt.

I looked around me. People were starting to pass out drunk; the sun was starting to rise. I needed to get the fuck away. To be alone and just breathe. I walked around the back of the property to the bike shop, instantly relaxing at the sight of it. I was a motorcycle mechanic. This was my shop. I'd missed it.

I stopped dead. My bike was standing by the side of the shop. My saddlebags full of my things. My tools, clothes, every-fucking-thing.

Tanner stood to the side, an empty whiskey bottle in his hand. A fucking lump threatened to block my throat. "Tann . . ." I said, but he just nodded his head once and tried to walk away. "Tann!"

He turned his head. "Go. Before I ain't got no choice but to put a fucking bullet through your skull."

"Tann . . ." I said again, but he wasn't saying fuck-all else. His flannel shirt was tied around his waist, revealing the swastika on the back of his sleeveless shirt. And I fucking watched him go until that swastika was out of sight.

My heart pounded. This was my one chance to get the fuck gone. I jumped on my bike and took the back route out of the ranch. I didn't look back. I just fucking rode, to where . . . it really didn't matter.

For the first time in my life, I was free.

CHAPTER TWO

Susan-Lee

"And your new Miss Central Texas is . . ." My cheeks ached from holding my fake-ass smile. My feet felt unsteady as the shoes I was wearing cut into my skin. But wearing heels two sizes too small would do that to a bitch.

I caught sight of my mamma, hands on her face as the presenter undid the envelope. "Miss Susan-Lee Stewart!"

Flashing lights from snapping cameras bombarded me, and confetti cannons burst in the air above the stage. I felt the disappointment from the other girls on the stage, their jealousy and sadness thick like smoke, clogging the air. Flowers were pushed into my hands, a sash draped around my pink dress, and a crown placed upon my head.

I grinned and waved like the robot my mamma had made me into. I saw her smiling up at me from the stage. Smiling like it was *her* who had won. Hell, it was. I could literally give two shits about this life.

My lips started to quake as the fake smile strained the muscles of my face. My eyes roved over the clapping crowd like I was seeing it from above, seeing it from another person's point of view. My heart pounded in my chest, and my head span.

What the hell am I doing here?

My feet stepped backward, then back again, until I spun around and fled from the stage. For once in my pathetic life I just ran, letting instinct take over. I ran and ran; even the torturous heels slicing into my feet didn't stop me.

"Susan-Lee! SUSAN!" I heard my mamma's voice from behind me. But there was no melting of the heart, no feeling guilty enough to stop. That bitch had made my life hell, and I was done. Her high-pitched shrill made me run that much faster, the bruise on my ribs pulsing with every step.

Seeing a fire exit sign, I hurried in that direction. I dropped the flowers to the floor, pushed on the bar, and rushed into the bright sun. I fled down the back alley and onto a small road. I searched left and right, my hand held out, praying for someone to stop.

I couldn't take one more damn day of that life. Another day of the dresses, the sunless tanner . . . and my mamma's fists.

Dread swarmed in my stomach when I heard my mamma's voice getting closer. Then the deafening roar of a motorcycle cut through the air. I frantically waved my hand for the guy to stop. I didn't think he would. Hope drained from me as I saw my mamma storming down the alley, her face like thunder and flushed with rage. It didn't matter that I was a grown-ass woman—she was my kryptonite. One I'd wasted too many years trying please, trying to make *love* me.

She was the only person who struck fear in me.

In my panic, my feet fumbled, my damn high heels causing my ankle to give way. I stumbled on the curb of the road and lurched forward. My hands reached out for something to break my fall, when my hip suddenly hit something hard, the flash of pain making me cry out. It only took me a few seconds to realize it was a motorcycle—a motorcycle that was slowly rolling to a stop beside me. Two hands took hold of my arms, and my head snapped up, only for my eyes to crash into a pair so blue they almost didn't look real. "Jesus! You almost ran me the fuck down!" I blurted, but my voice was barely above a whisper.

A huff of a laugh came from the lips of the blue-eyed biker. But his laugh faded when he looked over my shoulder and my mamma's voice sounded again. "You getting on or what, beauty queen? Looked like you were trying to hitch a ride."

I didn't need to look back at my mamma to help make my decision. I didn't even care that the guy was a unit with a shaved head, a massive red scar slicing down the side. I just saw my chance at freedom and damn well took it.

Climbing on the back of the Harley, I wrapped my arms around his waist and begged, "Please. Go!" We sped off. My heart slammed in my chest as the engine roared and the seat vibrated with power underneath me.

I glanced back, the venue fading from view. I tightened my arms around the guy's waist, and the smell of oil and leather surrounded me.

It smelled of freedom.

We drove. We rode and rode until the sun started to drop in the sky. I knew I should be worried. Especially when I saw the tattoos this guy was covered in. They were white power. I'd seen plenty of them in my life. He could be taking me anywhere. Could be a murderer or some shit. A trafficker. Yet I kept on holding on. That's how badly I needed away from my mamma.

I wasn't sure how many hours we'd been on the road, but we were no longer in Austin, that was for sure. At that realization I could suddenly breathe, the weight in my chest lifting for the first time in my life.

The guy took a left and pulled into a motel. The red neon sign buzzed, telling us they had rooms free. My legs felt numb as he parked up. My fingers were rigid, as if they'd been soldered to his waist. As the engine died, he sat there for a few minutes. I didn't move. Eventually, he looked at me. I had to swallow when those eyes met mine again. "You gonna move anytime today, beauty queen?"

I blinked, his slow drawl snapping me from my trance. I swung my leg from the saddle. As I stepped back, I really saw the guy for the first time. I swallowed on seeing the size of him, every inch of him covered in tattoos.

He was *gorgeous*.

His lip twitched as he looked at me. Then his gaze went to my head. It took me a minute to realize what he was laughing at. I ripped the crown from my head and threw it to the ground.

"Not a fan of crowns?"

"Fuck no," I spat back. His face lit up with humor. I held out my hand. "Susan-Lee."

He pushed his hand out and put it in mine. "Tank."

"I can see why you've got that name, sugar." I pulled my hand back. "Thanks for the rescue. It was much needed."

Tank nodded, then got off his bike. He looked even more intimidating standing up. Fuck. He looked *good*. The guy's face was beautiful. His eyes ran down my dress. "You ran from a pageant or some shit?"

I held out my arms. "Darlin', you're looking at the new Miss Central Texas." His eyes widened. "Or not.

I imagine my runaway stunt might mean I've officially abdicated from that title."

"You got money?" My face blanched. Tank didn't even let me reply that I hadn't. I hadn't thought of anything but fleeing that stage. A split-second decision. He reached into his leather jacket and handed me a wad of cash.

"I can't take that!"

"You're running. So the fuck am I. You'll need cash. I have it."

"Why are *you* running?" I blurted.

His face frosted over. He thrust the cash at me and forced it into my hand. "Take care, beauty queen." He turned and walked into the office. I followed. When I got inside, he was getting a key. He passed me with a nod and disappeared into one of the rooms outside.

"You want a room, sweetie?"

I looked at the woman behind the desk. "Yeah. Thanks."

Ten minutes later, I was looking at myself in the bathroom mirror. My hair was in such a state that if my mamma were here she would lose her ever-loving shit. I closed my eyes, feeling her phantom fist slam into my ribs at my lack of perfection.

When I opened my eyes again, I thrust my hands through my hair until every strand stuck up on end . . .

. . . and I laughed.

*****

I couldn't deny I liked the way the leather pants clung to my legs. Hell, I couldn't deny that they looked fucking good on me, period. The black tank clung to me like a second skin. Red lips and my hair down and straight finished the look off well. My new heels clicked on the sidewalk as I made my way to the bar at the side of the road. Country music spilled from the wooden walls, and neon signs for different brands of beer took up most of the windows.

I swung the door open and walked inside. It was half full, dark corners hiding most of the occupants. It wasn't my usual scene, but this mamma needed a damn drink, and here in the middle of nowhere, this was as good as I was gonna get.

I ignored the stares and the few wolf whistles that came my way. Tapping the bar, I said to the bartender, "Wine cooler if you have one, sugar."

"We got beer and whiskey, blondie."

I frowned. "Then a whiskey on the rocks." I hated whiskey. But right now I'd drink gasoline if I thought it would help me get wasted.

I slipped onto the stool as I waited for my drink. When it came I sipped at it, trying not to wince when it hit my tongue. I was one for a sweeter kind of liquor.

I felt someone sit beside me. Then a hand landed on my ass. I slowly placed my drink down then turned to face him. The guy was big and overweight and had a mustache. One sure-as-hell way to make a guy look like a creepy-ass fool—a fucking mustache.

Give me full stubble or a full beard any day. I couldn't deny how good that shit felt between my thighs.

His skin was covered in sweat. It nearly made me retch.

"You might wanna remove that hand from my ass, darlin'," I warned.

He smiled, and I wanted to spit in his face. "Kinda like where it's at."

I pushed his wrist, and his arm fell away. "Get. The. Fuck. Off."

I was turning back to my drink when his hand slapped my ass again. Harder this time. The impact made me spill my whiskey. The asshole wanted to hurt me, and I was about to lose my shit.

I swung, ready to rip this prick a new asshole, when an arm rested on the bar between me and him. "Get the fuck off her ass or I'll break your motherfucking jaw."

My eyes widened when I saw the familiar shaved head and scar.

"Fuck off, Nazi," the creep spat and tried to come at me again.

Tank didn't hesitate. He didn't speak again, just sent his fist into the creep's face, and the asshole hit the floor. But my stomach fell when a few other guys got to their feet. The creep clearly had friends. They charged at Tank. He just grinned and let fly with his huge fists. He made it look almost easy. Laughable. Until one of them grabbed a nearby bottle. Before I could do or say a damn thing, he smashed it over Tank's head. My heart thumped as I saw the blood sprout. My stomach fell and fear spread over my skin. Fear for Tank and what I'd gotten him into.

I shouldn't have started this shit.

Tank's punches were relentless. And even with blood trickling into his eyes, Tank fought the guys off until they were on the floor, groaning and covered in blood. When none of them made to get up again, he grabbed my hand and pulled me from the bar. I didn't look back; I was too busy fighting the funny sensation in my chest at the feel of Tank's roughened hand in mine. He took me to his bike. "Get on, beauty queen."

We pulled out from the bar and down the road to the motel. When we parked up, Tank looked back at me and sighed. "Why do I get the feeling you're trouble?"

I smiled and winked. Because I fucking was.

I slid from the motorcycle and tapped Tank's shoulder. "Come on, big boy. Gotta get you cleaned up."

"Nah, I'll do it—"

I swung to face him, hands on my hips. "Now I ain't gonna take no for an answer, darlin'. Get your hulking muscles off that bike and follow me." I ducked into the reception on the way. A young kid was behind the desk. Maybe sixteen. I leaned on the desk. His eyes immediately went to my tits. Always happened when you had a rack this size. Goddamn beacons on my chest. "You got a first aid kit I can borrow, sweetie?" The kid scrambled beneath the desk and put one on the top. "Thanks, darlin'."

Tank huffed a laugh behind me. "You'll be the one he jerks off to tonight," he muttered under his breath as I passed him.

I laughed, and saw something spark in Tank's blue eyes when I said, "Hope he ain't the only one."

He laughed louder. There went that damn light feeling in my chest again.

The blood on Tank's face made him look like something from a horror movie. I tapped his chest.

"Let's get that blood off your face before *you* give the kid nightmares."

I walked to my room. Tank followed. I could see the hesitation on his face when I looked back. He clearly didn't want to come with me.

Tough shit. He was coming.

As we entered my room, I pointed to the end of the bed. "Sit down. Shirt and jacket off."

Tank stalled. His jaw clenched. I was opening the first aid kit when I noticed. His eyes bored into the threadbare red carpet. I walked over and made him face me. "I've already seen the white power and Nazi tattoos, darlin'. So get the shirt and jacket off and show me those muscles. Those tats don't scare me. *You* don't scare me."

"I should."

I moved to the kit, ignoring his muttered words. It was a couple of minutes before I heard Tank sigh and start to shuck off his clothes. When I lifted my head, I was met with a wide chest littered with tattoo after tattoo. Scars were everywhere. White and red raised slashes, slicing through his black tattoos, making his skin look like a faded road map. No part of me thought Tank had had an easy life.

"You still in?" I asked as I guided him back to the bed. My hand barely covered even a quarter of his bicep. He was tall enough that his face was almost in line with mine when he sat down. He shook his head. I let out a quiet sigh of relief. He was out of the Klan.

We were quiet as I started wiping the blood from his head. There was a large gash on one side. On the opposite side to the shank scar. This close I could smell him again. He was like a walking extension of his bike—oil and leather and so damn good. The guy made my pussy clench. I was a sucker for the shaved-head, tattooed, muscled god look.

"You've been around the Klan?" Tank finally asked, his voice husky. His words snapped me out of my head.

"Family," I said. "Cousins and shit. I went to a few parties at their place in Waco as a teen." I shrugged. "Mamma and Papa were close to some Klansmen too. They weren't members on paper, of course, but they sure as shit would have killed me if I'd come home with a black or Mexican boyfriend." I looked down at Tank. "Papa died years ago, but Mamma probably would have approved of you."

"Good to know."

I poured some peroxide onto a cotton ball. "This will sting." I pressed the cotton ball to his cut. Tank didn't even flinch. But I did when his hands came to my waist. His thumbs ran over my hips. I could talk for Texas, but the touch of this guy took my voice the hell away.

Eventually I asked, "You get this scar with the Klan?"

Tank looked up at me. His hands stayed on my hips. "Prison."

I nodded. "You been out long?"

"Two days."

My eyes widened. "And you've already left the Klan?"

"Yesterday."

"Ah." Things were starting to make more sense. "You in prison long?"

"Three years."

I stepped back, moving to the cut on his cheek and lip. He'd taken a few punches to the face. "You want a drink?" I didn't even wait, just got the vodka from the mini fridge. I'd bought some supplies with some of the money Tank had given me. Well, I'd bought clothes and liquor.

Tank unscrewed the top and drank a few mouthfuls. He held the bottle out to me. "Shots? Always up for getting wasted, darlin'."

I followed suit, taking a few huge mouthfuls, then handed it back to him so I could work on his cuts. I could feel Tank's eyes on me the entire time. "There," I said and took another few swigs of vodka. I lifted my hand and stroked the shank scar.

"Prison fight?"

"More a Klan goodbye." My eyes widened. "Should've helped in a prison killing. I didn't. This was my reward."

"Shit, hon." I shook my head and sat down beside him. "So? The Klan after you now or something? Is that why you ran?"

"No. I have a buddy who helped me leave. My best friend. He got them all off my back. Didn't expect it." He took the vodka again and slugged it back. The room was starting to spin . . . I loved this feeling.

It made me horny as fuck.

I lay back on the bed. Tank looked at me and leaned back too, resting on his elbow. He had questions in his eyes. "You going back?"

"Fuck no," I said, and smiled when Tank immediately handed me back the bottle. I must have had a desperate-for-alcohol tone in my voice. I sipped at the good stuff and shuffled closer to Tank. I stared at a huge SS sign in the center of his chest. I reached out and traced the black lettering with my finger. His skin bumped under my touch. When I looked up at his face, he ran his tongue along his lower lip. I liked it. So I kept circling the letters. "My mamma is a psycho. She always has been. But it got worse when my papa died." I lifted my tank and showed him my stomach. Tank's eyes hooded at the sight of my body, and I saw his dick harden in his jeans . . . until I lifted it high enough for him to see. He froze when he saw the purple bruising. "It's amazing what makeup can cover these days." I licked my thumb and ran it down the side of my eye. I knew the makeup would've given way to that bruise too. Just as I was about to lower my top, Tank ran his fingers over the skin on my ribs.

I bit my lip, but not at the pain. It was at how much my pussy throbbed under his touch.

Those fingers, the vodka, and the sight of his muscles and tattoos were fucking turning me on. I was a girl with a healthy appetite. Liked to get my pussy stroked and filled. And right now, I was getting real messed-up thoughts about Tank.

"Why did you stay?"

I shrugged. "I didn't want her to be alone after Papa. His death destroyed her. She had a shitty life growing up. Wasn't much better as an adult. I wanted to make it better for her. She wanted me to be Miss America so bad. So I went along with it all to make her happy. Devoted my life to it, hoping she'd just love me, treat me better." But that sympathy I'd once felt for her no longer existed. "Now I'm done giving a shit. That bitch can rot in hell. There are only so many chances someone can have before they deserve nothing else." Tank's fingers started moving across my stomach . . . and lower. My breathing hitched. "You going somewhere with that finger there, darlin'?"

His lip kicked up at the side. "You're fucking beautiful, beauty queen."

I took hold of his hand and sat up. Tank watched every movement I made. The guy had been locked up for three years. He got out two days ago. He must have been bursting for a fuck.

I kissed each finger, then, when his mouth was just an inch from mine, pushed his hand to the crotch of my jeans and said, "I like having my stomach stroked as much as the next girl, darlin', but I'd rather feel those fingers all up in my pussy."

Tank paused, his mouth parting at my words. Then he did exactly as I said. He ran his fingers over my jeans, cupping my pussy through the denim, the feel of his fingers between my legs sending shivers all over my body. I hooked my hand around the back of his neck, and our mouths crashed together. I tasted the slight tinniness of blood on my tongue, but it disappeared, taken over by tobacco and liquor. Tank didn't give me the control for long. He rolled me onto my back and smothered me with his huge muscles. I wrapped my legs around his waist, arms clasped around his neck. Tank's tongue fought against mine, our breathing heavy.

The alcohol sailed through my veins. Breaking from his mouth, I moved to straddle him. He smiled as I sat on his waist and looked down. "How old are you, darlin'?"

Tank smirked. "You think I'm jailbait?"

I crawled over his naked torso. Tank groaned and gritted his teeth at the sight. "Twenty-three."

I smiled. "Then I hope you like older women."

Tank grabbed my waist and flipped me onto my back again. "Fucking love 'em." Then he kissed me. Tank's lips were soft against mine. It surprised me how soft. He was so big and rough, with that deep graveled voice. He tasted of mint and liquor.

I was instantly addicted.

Tank broke away from my mouth, leaving me desperate to have him back. He smirked, clearly seeing my need for his taste back in my mouth. But he didn't kiss me again; instead, he pulled my tank over my head to reveal the black bra that barely held my tits. "Fuck," he groaned. He cupped one breast with his hand, then reached between them to unhook the front fastening.

Damn, he knew what he was doing.

My tits sprang free, and he immediately took my right nipple into his mouth. I held him tighter as the wet lashes of his tongue made me moan. His dick rubbed against my clit.

He was driving me crazy.

"Get my jeans off," I said. Tank's hands moved to my waistband and snapped open the buttons. I lifted my ass so he could pull them down. He took my black thong with them. He must have agreed that there was no time to admire my fucking underwear—though they *were* sexy as fuck.

I kicked off my jeans and felt Tank's fingers slip along my pussy lips. Shudders ran down my spine. But I needed him naked too. I unfastened his jeans and pushed them down. I licked my lips when his long thick cock slapped against his stomach.

"Shit, darlin'. You're hung!"

Tank clearly wasn't in the mood for chatting about his dick's girth. He shuffled down the bed and spread my legs apart with his calloused hands. His eyes locked on my pussy as his fingers circled my clit. I put my hand on the back of his head, just in case he tried to go anywhere else. "So fucking pretty," he rasped, and then swiped his hot tongue from my slit to my clit. My back arched off the bed. But he didn't stop. He just kept going, lapping his tongue over my clit and up inside me, making me lose my fucking mind.

"Tank . . . fuck," I cried out as my legs started to shake.

"You taste fucking perfect, beauty queen." He pushed two fingers inside me. I bucked and thrashed on the mattress. My nails dug into Tank's shaven scalp, but he didn't even flinch. "Gonna come, darlin'," I hushed out as his tongue worked my clit and his fingers hit my G-spot. My legs shook harder and my eyes closed as I broke apart, my orgasm taking over my whole body. Tank didn't stop, just kept licking until I pushed his head away, laughing and calling out when I couldn't take any more.

"Enough!" I screamed. Tank moved away to take another shot from the vodka bottle that had been discarded on the bed beside us. He took another, then climbed over me, holding the vodka in his mouth. He brought his mouth to mine. The minute I opened my lips, vodka filled my mouth and trickled down my throat. I barely got time to swallow before his tongue was in my mouth, thrashing against mine. I moaned; I was getting wetter by the second.

I pushed Tank's chest and guided him to his back. I reached for the vodka and took three long mouthfuls. I poured a shot into Tank's mouth, returning the favor, then poured a stream of liquor onto his ripped stomach. The vodka pooled at his abs. Moaning at the sight, I lowered my head. I lapped at the vodka with my tongue, before sipping my way up his abs to his wide chest. My lips curved into a smile when I saw him looking down at me, his arms folded behind his head.

But his quick breathing told me he wasn't as calm as he looked.

"Feels fucking good, beauty queen." His pupils were blown.

I ducked my head back down and nipped and licked my way down to his dick. I paused as I reached the tip, the head already wet from the vodka. Tank's chest rose and fell in anticipation. Without breaking eye contact, I licked the flat of my tongue over his cock, lapping a lazy circle around the head. "Fuck!" Tank hissed, and fisted his hand in my hair. I felt fucking high. The vodka, the freedom, and the fact I had this beast of a guy breathless under me had me high as a kite.

With short, gentle licks, I teased and teased until Tank's thigh muscles were strained. "Beauty . . ." he rasped, unable to finish the sentence with his usual "queen." I liked it better. His hand gripped my hair so tight I moaned. "Beauty . . ." Tank said again. "Beauty—"

His words cut off as I swallowed his cock, taking him right to the back of my throat. "Shit," he groaned, bucking his hips, making me take more of him. I took it. Sucking, swirling my tongue around the tip and along the veins and ridges. And I didn't let up. I worked him faster and faster with every passing second. I couldn't get enough of his taste on my tongue, and I swallowed every bit of pre-cum that burst in my mouth.

"Fuck." Tank pushed my head from his dick. "I'm gonna come if you don't stop." I kept going, addicted to his taste. "No," he said, then picked me up as if I weighed nothing. He crushed his mouth to mine. "Wanna fuck you, beauty queen. Wanna be inside that hot cunt when I come."

I wrapped my legs around his waist and rolled my pussy against his hard cock. "Then fuck me and stop just fucking talking about it."

Tank growled, then reached over to his discarded jeans and pulled out a rubber. I held on to him, my arms around his neck, as he tore the wrapper. I lay back on the mattress, legs open and waiting while he rolled the rubber down his big dick. He crawled over me then flipped me onto my stomach.

I called out in surprise, smiling when I fell to the mattress beneath me. Tank's arms hooked under my shoulders and his mouth came to my ear. "Get ready, beauty queen."

I opened my legs wide and turned my head, speaking against his lips. "*You* get ready, big boy. You ain't ever had a pussy as tight as mine."

Tank smirked at my sass, then slammed into me in one long stroke. I groaned, my forehead dropping to the mattress. "Fuck!" Tank's heavy weight pressed against me, his hard stomach to my back. And he did as he promised. He didn't let up. He fucked me into the mattress. It wasn't slow and steady; it was primal and raw and fucking savage . . . exactly what I needed.

The liquor in my stomach made my head swim. I clutched the pillows as moan after moan slipped from my lips, joining Tank's groans. I rolled my hips, giving back as much as I received. Tank tightened his grip on me, then suddenly pulled out and rolled me over, only to hitch my legs over his shoulders and sink back into me again.

"Christ! Yes!" I moaned, my head snapping back as my legs started to shake. Tank's hands moved to my tits, squeezing the flesh on his palms. "These tits . . ." he growled, thrusting faster as I clenched around his dick.

"I'm gonna come . . ." I said, my hands gripping the headboard as he relentlessly took me, harder and harder until I didn't know my own fucking name. Tank pounded into me one more time, then I stilled and let my orgasm rip through me. I dropped my hands and dug my nails into him so hard that I cut into his tattooed skin. I opened my eyes to see Tank's eyes close and his teeth clench.

He slammed into me one last time and came, a long, groaned "Fuck!" slipping from his lips.

I couldn't take my eyes off him as he rocked into me, slowing with every thrust. Couldn't rip my eyes from his as they opened and I caught sight of that bright blue. He caught his breath as he stared down at me, a smile pulling on his lips.

"You got a sweet pussy, beauty queen." He smiled wider. "That was worth three years of waiting."

I laughed, shivers spreading on my skin from the feel of him still inside me. "And you got a sweet cock, darlin'."

Tank leaned down and kissed me, laughing against my lips. He slipped from me and lay beside me. I rolled to face him, tracing a skull tattoo on his arm. His skin was wet with sweat and liquor. "Any vodka left?" I asked.

He grabbed the bottle from the floor. There was a mouthful for each of us at the bottom. We each took a shot, and he threw the bottle to the floor. Tank rolled his head on the pillow to face me. "I thought beauty queens were meant to be all prim and proper. Not taking on convicted Klan members in the sack and talking dirty about pussies and cocks."

I leaned up on my elbow. "Firstly, *ex*-Klan members. And secondly, I ain't no beauty queen anymore. You gotta cut that nickname right the fuck now."

He smirked. "I'll just stick with Beauty then."

I rolled my eyes, but I kinda loved that. Beat Susan-fucking-Lee. I leaned my arms on Tank's chest. "I might've been a beauty queen, but I was no angel." I laughed. "Let's just say that from a young age I learned to sneak outta my window and get my fun. The beauty-queen shit was all a mask I wore for my mamma. I ain't no Virgin Mary. I like sex and I ain't ashamed to say so."

"When you were young . . . ?" Tank said. "And when was that?"

"Ah." I nodded. "You wanna know how old I am?" Tank shrugged. "Forty," I said, and watched his eyes widen. I paused for a second, until I let my laugh free and rolled onto my back. "Shit, darlin', you shoulda seen your face!"

Tank pinned my arms above my head and smothered my body so I couldn't move. There was light in his expression. It was a nice change. There seemed to be a whole world of darkness hiding behind those bright blue eyes. "How old?" He rubbed his semi-hard cock along my pussy lips, making me shiver.

He was addictive.

I bit my lip as heat flooded my pussy again. When he moved away, I reached out to wrap my arms around his waist, fighting to bring him back to finish what he'd just started. He cocked his eyebrow, his huge body not moving an inch, waiting for me to answer. "Fine!" I said. "Twenty-five! I'm twenty-five."

Tank rolled off me. Though his hand stayed on my stomach. Possessively. I liked it. "Only two years then. Hardly a cougar."

I shrugged. "It was fun to bust your balls."

Tank grabbed my arms, launched me to his mouth, then let me down again. I smiled, liking that he wanted to kiss me. "So what will you do now?"

Tank sighed, and his eyebrows pinched together. The darkness that I could see lived inside him was back, simmering under his bright eyes. "No fucking idea. Keep moving on for a while. Give my ex-brothers some time to forget about me." I wondered what stories he had from his days in the Klan. Wondered what he'd done, what played on his mind. Why he left.

What he did to put him in prison.

Lying here now, I couldn't imagine him doing anything bad. But the way he'd handled the creep and his friends at the bar told me he was lethal under that sweet-ass smirk.

"Your mamma was bad to you?" His question caught me off guard. I nodded, wondering where he was going with this. "You're twenty-five . . ." His words trailed off to nothing. But I got the subtext. *Why the fuck did you stay?*

The vodka suddenly seemed completely gone from my system. "Because I loved her." I laughed, but there was fuck-all humor in it. "*Love* her." I sighed. "But she is a leech. All she ever does is take. I'm not even sure why the hell she wanted a kid. Maybe to live her life through me. The failed beauty queen." Tank brushed back my hair. "When my papa died, I think the last speck of goodness in her did too. There wasn't much there to begin with." I looked out to nothing. "But she was all I had left, so I stayed." I shook my head. "But up on that stage yesterday . . . I don't know what happened. I'd just had enough. I saw her face, felt the bruises I'd spent hours hiding, and just knew I was done. She'll be alone . . . but I can't imagine ever going back. She doesn't deserve me to."

A minute or two of silence followed.

"You have a big heart, Beauty."

I swallowed, but then I looked him dead in the eyes. "And you have a big cock."

Tank's eyes widened, but he fought a smile. "Both good things."

"Amen!" He laughed. "Sooo . . ." I dropped my head to the side. "You want some company as you travel around just 'moving on'?" My heart suddenly beat fast in my chest, and I realized I was nervous for his answer. And I knew why. Deep down, I really didn't want to be alone, as much as I talked the talk.

I thought—more *hoped*—maybe he didn't either.

"I ain't a good man," he said, his face clouding over with an expression that told me it was the truth. The light had faded from his blue eyes and his lips had thinned.

I studied him. Really studied him. The scar, the tattoos, the white-power shit that I knew should bother me . . . but he said he'd left. Which told me there was more to him than he thought. And I thought back to tonight, to the bar, to how he came to my rescue.

"I've just fucked you a day after meeting you. Maybe I'm not such a good girl."

"You are," he said immediately. "You're good."

A lump clogged my throat. I didn't know why, but I linked my fingers through his. I brought the back of his hand to my lips and kissed the scarred skin. Not letting go of his hand, I climbed to straddle his lap.

Tank's free hand cupped my ass, keeping me in place. He looked right in my eyes. "I'm coming with you," I said. I leaned forward and kissed his lip, which was starting to bruise from the fight in the bar. I shrugged. "The way I see it, I get protection from a savage, muscled god, and you get free pussy on tap. What's there to consider?"

Tank's hand tightened in mine, and a smirk eventually pulled on his soft lips. "Nothing," he sighed, shaking his head. "Nothing the fuck at all."

I laughed and ran my bare pussy along his thickening dick. "Then how about a celebratory fuck?"

Tank flipped me on my back, rubbed my clit with his finger, and said, "Best fucking thing to ever come out your pretty-ass mouth."

So we fucked.

CHAPTER THREE

Tank

Four months later . . .

I rolled my bike to a stop outside the diner and peered inside the long silver trailer. A wide smile greeted me from the nearest window. I flicked my chin and felt that fire rush through my chest, the one I'd felt every fucking day for four months. A minute later the door swung open and a fucking bombshell in a tight pink waitress uniform strutted out of the diner and down the steps that led her to me.

Arms came around my neck and a pair of red lips smashed against mine. "Darlin'," Beauty whispered against my mouth.

I slapped her ass. "Get the fuck on. We're riding today."

Beauty straddled the back of my bike and wrapped her arms around my waist. Her tongue traced the shell of my ear. I tightened my hands on the handlebars as my cock pushed against my jeans. Bitch got me hard every fucking time she touched me.

And she knew it. The woman could be a total cocktease.

I reached behind me and moved my hand straight to her pussy. Beauty moaned into my mouth. I pulled my hand away and made sure her blue eyes were locked on mine as I licked along each finger. She moaned and bit her lip. Grabbing hold of my face, she kissed me hard. "I can never get enough of you."

I smirked and turned back to my bike. Kicking up the kickstand, I pulled out onto the road, feeling Beauty's big tits pressing against my back.

She said she couldn't get enough of me, but I couldn't fucking quit the woman. Since the night of the bar fight, she'd never left my side. Staying in hickville towns a few weeks at a time, grabbing work where we could, just moving, riding, and fucking. Her and her long-ass red nails had clawed their way into my fucked-up soul.

My woman was going no-fucking-where.

Beauty gripped me tighter as I built up speed, rushing by the bike shop I'd managed to get some work at. It was a shithole, and the bikes that came through weren't no good to work on. But we'd be out of here soon, off to whatever town we rolled up in.

We rode for an hour, ending up at a rest stop in the middle of fucking nowhere. "I need a piss, darlin'!" Beauty shouted into my ear. I rolled my eyes as she climbed off the bike the minute I stopped and strutted, high heels clicking on the pavement, to the rundown building.

I lit up a smoke and took a drag, then I saw a guy on the other side of the rest stop. He was a big fucker wearing a leather cut, with long dark hair, and a smoke in his hand. He was leaning against a Fat Boy Harley, and I almost got hard at how fucking beautiful that machine was.

Smoke was billowing from the engine. "Fucking cunt!" the guy shouted and threw his cell. It smashed to the floor. I looked over at the bathroom. There was no sign of Beauty. I walked toward the guy and his bike. Out here, there was fuck-all cell service. He was stuck.

And I'd have given my left nut to work on a bike like that.

I was only a few feet away when he pulled a gun, his crazy fucking hazel eyes staring me down. "One more step, Nazi cunt, and I'll blow a motherfuckin' slug through your skull."

As I lifted my hands up, I saw his cut. *Fuck*. The Hades Hangmen. And not just any member, but the fucking prez of the Austin chapter. The mother chapter.

Psycho cracked his neck from side to side, gun still held out. His eyes never left me as he carried on smoking as if he wasn't about to kill me on the spot. He flicked the butt to the ground. "Who sent you?" he asked, voice fucking laced with death.

Reaper, his cut read. *Reaper Nash.*

I kept my cool. "No one sent me. I ain't with the Klan anymore."

Reaper raised his eyebrow. "Your ink says otherwise." His eyes narrowed. "Thought you could get me alone? Could cut me down without my brothers?" He smiled, but it was cold as fuck. He stepped closer and closer until the barrel of his Glock pressed against the middle of my forehead. "Got news for you, Klan fucker. You ain't gonna kill me. I murder pieces of shit like you just for fuckin' Sunday mornin' fun."

"I ain't lying." I swallowed. "Used to be with the Klan . . ." I paused, but then thought I might as well tell him. "Austin. But left four months ago. Ain't going back."

His hazel eyes flared. "One of Landry's?" I nodded. "Why did you leave?"

"Fucking hate the cunt."

Reaper assessed me, never moving his gun. "You got intel on them?" His head cocked to the side. "You know Landry gets out soon." My stomach fell. I didn't wanna say shit about my old brotherhood. Tanner . . . I wouldn't betray my best friend that way.

"Saw you had bike trouble. I'm a mechanic. Harley specialist." I jerked my chin to his bike. Reaper stared at me, and fuck if I didn't see the promise of death in his eyes.

"Tank?" Beauty's voice came from behind me. It was shaking.

"Who the fuck is this slut?"

Anger ripped through me. "My old lady," I said through gritted teeth. I knew enough about the fucking Hangmen to know to immediately own my woman. I didn't look back but said, "It's all right, baby. Stay back."

I had no fucking idea if Reaper believed a word I said, but he pulled back his Glock and nudged his head in the direction of his bike. "Fix it. Then we'll see if I let you live or not." He smiled, a sick and fucked-up smile. "If you fuck up, you'll just be another of my donations to the boatman."

"Beauty, get my tools from my bike." Beauty's heels clicked across the ground. When she handed the tools to me, I saw the tears in her eyes. "It'll be okay," I said, not knowing if that shit was true. I flicked my chin, telling her to get back. To keep away.

I looked over my shoulder at Reaper, who'd lit up another smoke. He held his Glock by his side, ready to send me to Hades. I bent down and in minutes found the problem. "Your fuel injector is fucked."

Reaper didn't say shit for a second. Then, "Fix it."

I closed my eyes and took a deep breath. I glanced up at Beauty. There was no fucking way I was losing her. It could be fixed enough for him to get home. But I knew about Reaper. A fucking cold-blooded killer. Killed for fun, and he'd made the Hangmen mother chapter the most fucking violent and feared gang in all of Texas. Fuck, in all of the States. Landry never went near the Hangmen for a reason.

Rumor had it the cunt even killed his own old lady in front of his mute kid.

My life could depend on how pissed the fucker was in this second.

I got to work. An hour later, the bike was patched up. I stood up and stepped back. Reaper walked, calm as fuck, to the bike and bent down, looking at my work. I was good. Real fucking good. I knew it would be the best work he'd ever seen.

Reaper stood back up and breathed the smoke from his cigarette in my face. He started the engine. The Fat Boy purred. I lifted my eyebrow. "Midday tomorrow. Hangmen compound. Be there." Reaper looked back at Beauty. "Leave Big Tits the fuck at home."

"Ain't planning on going back to Austin."

Reaper smiled. It was anything but a good smile. "Wasn't fucking asking, Nazi. I'm in the business of *tellin'*, and I'm tellin' you to get your Nazi ass to the compound tomorrow." He put another smoke in his mouth and took a swig of the bourbon that had been in his saddlebag. "No one touches the Hangmen or anyone on our compound, if you're being a weepin' pussy over your old brotherhood seeing you." His smile got wider. Crazier. "Though I always fucking enjoy it when they try."

He flew down the road back to Austin. I sucked in a quick breath and turned. Beauty launched herself into my arms. Her legs wrapped around my waist and her arms were tight around my neck. "It's all right, baby," I said, but I felt her tears against my neck. She didn't let go. Instead she pulled back, giving me a glimpse of her watering blue eyes, then smashed her lips to mine. Her long red nails clawed at my jacket, then my shirt. I walked forward until I had her against the wall.

Her hand ran over my cock and I groaned into her mouth. She was desperate, fucking frenzied as she fumbled with my zipper and pulled out my cock. I didn't wait. I pushed her panties aside and slid the fuck in. Beauty's head snapped back as I pounded into her. Her moans sailed around the deserted rest stop. I crushed my lips to hers and fucking groaned when her tongue pushed into my mouth.

I fucked Beauty hard, her pussy gripping my cock. My head fell to her shoulder as she came, her tight pussy taking me over with her. I slammed into her three more times before she sagged in my arms. Sweat ran down my back. I looked up at Beauty. Her hands were immediately on my face, and my heart fucking broke when I saw the tears on her cheeks.

I went to say something, to tell her it was okay, when she whispered, "I love you." My breath got caught in my chest. "You know that? I've fucking fallen in love with you, darlin'."

"I know." I held her tighter. "Love you too, beauty queen."

She laughed at her old nickname, but then the tears started falling again. "I was so scared," she whispered.

"It's my life, baby." Beauty blinked up at me. I pulled out from her pussy and pushed her panties back in place. Before I could let her go, Beauty reached down and put me back in my jeans, fastening them back up.

"I didn't want you to let me go."

Fuck . . . this woman . . .

Gripping her tighter, I inhaled her flowery scent. "You didn't know me when I was in the Klan." I took a long fucking breath. "I've killed before. You know that, right?" I hadn't told her why I'd been in prison. Hadn't really told her anything about my past.

Beauty's eyes widened, but then her shoulders sagged. "Yeah . . . I know."

I picked Beauty up and carried her to the edge of the land behind the rest stop. I slumped against a tree, keeping her in my lap. She laid her head on my chest. "I miss it," I said, and Beauty froze.

She looked into my eyes. "The Klan?" Her voice was thick with fear.

"Being in a brotherhood." Sympathy quickly replaced the panic on her face. "I ain't made for this life, jumping between towns, alone." Beauty's face paled, and she moved to get up. I stopped her. "*We* ain't. You got too big a personality to be trapped in this kind of life. No friends."

"I want *you*."

"You got me. Always." I took hold of her hand. "But we're going to Austin."

Beauty stared off into the woods behind us. "I know of the Hangmen, Tank. They're fucking insane." She ran her hand over my forehead, then kissed the center. "That asshole had a gun to your head."

I couldn't help but smirk. "That asshole is the meanest motherfucker I've ever heard of."

"And we're going to them tomorrow anyway?"

We. 'Cause she was never going anywhere without me again. "Fucking Reaper Nash tells you to be somewhere, you arrive an hour early with a fucking smile on your face. I ain't messing with the Hangmen. They have a bike shop. Maybe that's it. Maybe there'll be an offer of a job."

Beauty got to her feet, then stared down at me for a few seconds. "Then we got a long journey back to the ATX." I got up and kissed her lips. "I need to pick up my things from the motel and change into my leathers."

As she went to walk to the bike, I pulled her back to me, her tits pushed against my chest. I took her chin with my free hand. "But the panties stay on. Wanna know my cum is still inside you when we ride."

"Careful, darlin'," she warned as she broke from me and strutted toward the bike. She looked back at me over her shoulder. "Or ain't no one making it to Austin tomorrow."

I smiled, then got on my bike and took us to pick up our shit. We had an appointment with the Reaper to keep.

*****

I stared up at the building, a painting of Hades, the Hangmen emblem, staring back at me. The gate opened and I walked through. A few guys were scattered around the yard. This was the bike shop's entrance. No fucker got through the main entrance unless you were patched in. Found that out when I'd first joined the Klan and a bunch of newbies thought they could take on this club. Wanted to get into Landry's good graces. Not one of those assholes came back alive. Reaper sent the security tape of them being beaten to death by him and his VP to the ranch for our enjoyment.

"You're the Nazi?"

I snapped my head to the side to see a huge fuck-off Samoan-looking guy glaring at me. His had ink everywhere, even on his face. He wore jeans and a wifebeater. Both were covered in oil.

"Ex," I said and stared at the fucker right back. He raised his eyebrow like he didn't believe one word I said.

"Reaper said you fixed his bike." It wasn't a question. The Samoan walked off, and I followed. I walked past some fucker with long red hair, who sent me a Nazi salute as I passed then blew me a kiss.

Prick.

We arrived at the garage, where three Harleys sat. The Samoan pointed at a Street Glide in the corner. "You fix that by the end of the day, you got a job." Excitement fucking burst in my veins. The guy walked to the Fat Boy across the shop. It was almost identical to the one Reaper rode yesterday.

I looked up. "You got a name?"

The guy looked back. "Not fucking white."

I sighed, then got my tools from my bike and got the fuck to work.

The Samoan checked all around the bike. When he

stood up, he eyed me with death in his gaze. "You got a problem with anyone outside the supreme white race or whatever the fuck you cunts claim to be?"

"I did. Then didn't. Did time. Then walked the fuck away." I instinctively ran my hand over my shank scar. The Samoan's eyes narrowed on the movement.

He stepped closer. "You cross Reaper, or any of us brothers, and it'll be you who gets lynched. I don't give a fuck how good a mechanic you are. You're here to work. You hear anything you shouldn't, you keep your head the fuck down and don't repeat a word." He paused. "And we find out anything about us gets to those Klan cunts of Landry's, your old boys, I'll personally cut out your tongue and mail it to your old lady so she knows you won't be licking her pussy no more."

"Understood."

He moved back to the Street Glide. "Never seen work as good as this . . . not even my own."

"That hard for you to admit?" I crossed my arms across my chest.

The Samoan raised his brow at me. "Fuck yeah." I smirked. "Bull." I frowned.

"I'm Bull. I run this shop. But I'm in desperate need of a mechanic who's A, good, and B, not a fucking pussy around my brothers and the shit that goes down around here."

I nodded my head, about to say something when a voice came from the entrance of the workshop. "He work out or do I have to send him to the boatman?" Reaper walked in. As yesterday, the fucker had the promise of a real fucking slow and painful death in his eyes. A kid walked behind him. He looked like Reaper, but younger.

The kid watched me with the same suspicious eyes as his old man.

"He'll do," Bull said.

"You got the job," Reaper told me. But I could see by the disappointment on his face that he'd rather have had an excuse to kill me. Reaper looked at Bull. "His bike done?" He nudged his head to the kid behind him. Looked eighteen, nineteen. Something like that.

"Just finished."

Bull showed Reaper the bike. The kid looked over his shoulder, looking up at me, eyes suspicious. "Nice ink," I said. He had a picture of Hades and his old lady on his arm, like the mural I'd seen out in the yard. Two bright-as-fuck blue eyes stood out on the woman. "Been doing tattoos since I was a kid. I'm good, but that work's better," I added.

The kid nodded. Reaper let out a loud laugh. "Won't get nothing from my retarded kid. Doesn't speak." The kid clenched his jaw. Reaper put his arm around the kid's shoulder and put his hand on his son's jaw. "Styx here 'signs,' whatever the fuck that shit is." Reaper started moving Styx's jaw like he was talking, like he was a fucking puppet and Reaper was the puppet master. "My name's Styx and I'm a fucking pussy. Take after my cunt of a mamma." Styx just stood there and let the fucker do it. Reaper laughed then pointed at me as he started walking out, Styx following behind. "Bull here tells you what the fuck to do. Do it, and I won't have to kill you." He shook his head. "And for fuck's sake, cover up the fucking Nazi ink. Makes me wanna peel your skin off you when I see it, and I really don't wanna lose a good mechanic. Try Hades shit as a cover-up."

Reaper walked out, and Bull got the fuck to work. He glanced up from the desk he'd slipped behind. "Be here tomorrow. Eight a.m."

Twenty minutes later I walked into the motel room we'd gotten last night. The door hadn't even closed before Beauty was in my fucking arms, her legs around my waist as usual. Her lips crashed to mine. When she pulled back, she checked every inch of my face. "You okay?" she asked, her eyes wide. "They didn't hurt you?"

I smiled, then, gripping her ass, lowered us to sit on the bed. "I'm good, baby." She let out a huge breath. I palmed her tight, full ass.

"Shit, darlin'. I've been a wreck all day." She laughed, but I could hear the shake in her voice. Fucking destroyed me.

I kissed her, and she kissed me back like it was the last time I'd ever see her. "I got a job," I said. She blinked at me, then nodded. I sighed and dropped my forehead to hers. "I ain't a good guy, baby. I know you know it. But this is who I am. I ain't ever gonna walk the straight and narrow. Klan, Hangmen—I belong in that fucked-up world." When I looked up at her, I said, "You and me? We've been living in a fucking bubble for months. But it had to burst at some point. I was always gonna be dragged into this kind of fucking life." My stomach pulled, pains shooting inside like I was being shivved. I decided to tell her everything. My past. What I'd done. Why I'd been sent to prison. Beauty was stock still with every word I spoke.

Unable to read her, what the fuck she thought of what I'd done, I said, "You know it all. Now you gotta decide if you're in." I held her tighter, just in case it was the last time. "You're good, Beauty. You can go somewhere. Get a better man. You need to decide—"

"You," she said before I'd even finished. "I choose you. You're not the man you used to be." She straightened her back. "I get you ain't ever gonna walk the straight and narrow. May do bad shit again. But I'm not a pussy, Tank. I got this. Got you. I can live this life."

A smile tugged on my lips at the determination in her eyes. Then it fell. "If the Klan find out I got a job with the Hangmen, it could cause shit." I paused. "Real shit." I shook my head. "There could be a hit on me. I ain't stupid. If the Klan think I've joined the Hangmen, it could put a huge fucking target on my head." My stomach sank. "Could put one on you too." I squeezed my eyes shut, trying to fucking breathe. "It isn't safe to be with me. Beauty . . . I don't think—"

"Don't," she snapped. She put her hands on my cheeks. "Don't fucking try to make my decisions for me. My psycho mamma tried to do that to me. I sure as shit won't have my man do it too." She rolled her hips, her pussy running along my cock. Her lips went to my ear. "I'm in. And I can handle myself." She dragged her lips along my cheek until they hit my lips. "I got you, darlin'. 'Til the end." She crushed her lips to mine. "Now shut the hell up so I can fuck you. All that worrying has made me hungry for your cock." I laughed when Beauty pushed me down to the bed and in a couple of seconds had my zipper down. My cock out and down the back of her throat.

Bitch wasn't going anywhere.

CHAPTER FOUR

Beauty

Two months later . . .

The compound was massive. I clutched Tank's waist as he rode through the gate. We came to a stop outside a building with a huge-ass picture of Hades and Persephone on a wall. I'd been doing some reading up.

I wouldn't let Tank see my nerves as I heard the music blasting through the walls. When I turned my head, some young guy with long blond hair was fucking some girl up against the wall. Screwing her in the open where anyone could see.

Tank got off the bike and took my hand. He smiled when he followed my gaze, like it was nothing out of the ordinary. "You ready?" The guy who was fucking groaned, clearly coming, then stood off the wall and fastened his zipper.

"Tank," he said and flicked up his chin. His blue eyes fell on me. "Sweet cheeks."

"Ky," Tank greeted, then pointed at me. "Beauty. My old lady." Ky lit up a smoke and came over to us.

"Beauty." He looked at my chest. I was wearing red leathers and my favorite black tank. "Nice tits."

My head cocked to the side. I gestured at the wall he'd just been fucking against. "Nice technique."

Ky fucking blinded me with a beautiful smile, then pointed at Tank. "She's a keeper. Spots real talent when she sees it." He strutted off back inside, but called back, "You ever get sick of our 'roided-up Nazi mechanic here, you give me a call. You'll be creamin' more than you've ever creamed in your life."

"Good to know," I said, and he disappeared through a door. I turned to Tank and raised an eyebrow.

"Ky Willis. VP's kid. Resident slut."

I stared at the door he'd just gone through. "Fuck. That kid's prettier than me. Bastard."

Laughing, Tank threw his arm around my shoulders. "Stick to me tonight. I ain't patched in. That means you're free pussy. But I know all the brothers. They see you with me, they shouldn't try anything."

I nodded. Tank had told me some of the club rules. It was a different world here. I'd never been to a Saturday at the club before. But over the last couple of months Tank had grown closer to the men here. I wasn't stupid. I knew he secretly wanted to be patched in. Knew he wanted to become a Hangmen prospect. I had no fucking idea about this club or what Reaper was looking for in a brother, but I couldn't imagine it wouldn't happen for Tank at some point. If they could get past the fact he was ex-Klan, that is.

Making me the old lady of a Hangman.

I knew I needed to prove myself tonight too.

Tank held me tighter as we entered the clubhouse. My feet faltered a little when the door to the bar opened and I took in the scene. The air was thick with smoke, music pounding from the speakers. Hangmen were scattered all over the room, most with their hands and mouths busy with almost-naked—and some fully naked—women writhing all over them. "You okay?" Tank asked in my ear.

I nodded. But *shit* . . . I wasn't sure I was.

"Tank!" A voice cut through the noise. A mountain of a man with long black hair and tribal tattoos all over his face and body was waving us over. Bull. I knew by looking at him that this was who Tank worked with. Tank didn't say much, but I knew he considered Bull a friend. I wasn't sure if Bull felt the same. Wasn't sure if any if these men could ever truly get over Tank's Klan past.

Tank led us through the crowd. Suddenly, two men were in front of us. I despised one on sight. "Reaper," Tank greeted. His arm tightened around my shoulders. "Big Poppa," he said to the other guy.

"This a slut?" the one Tank called Big Poppa asked.

"My old lady," Tank replied.

"Fuck, maybe I should've been a Klansmen if I got a slut with tits and ass like that." My head whipped to the side as another mountain, this time with red hair, came up beside us.

"Vike," Tank said, gritting his teeth.

This "Vike's" eyes stayed on my chest. "Real or fake?" My mouth dropped open in shock. "No, don't tell me." He stared at my tits for another minute before clicking his fingers. "Fake. Dr. Turnbull, right? I'd know his work anywhere."

I broke from Tank. He tried to hold on, but instead I walked the few inches to Vike. I palmed my tits in both hands and said, "All real, darlin'. Tank's a fucking lucky guy."

Vike's eyes widened and he groaned. "Tank," he said, pointing at Tank's face. "I really fuckin' hate you right now." Vike rubbed his hand over his dick. He looked around the room. "Now I gotta get some slut to tit-fuck my anaconda so I can picture myself coming all over yours." He shook his head. "Bitch, I was just gonna do some tequila shots too." He shrugged. "But when the anaconda needs feeding . . ." With that he was off across the room, grabbing a big-titted blonde and pushing her hand straight to his cock. The girl's face lit up like it was Christmas and the big red giant was Santa Claus.

Idiot.

Reaper and Big Poppa had walked off. Tank led me to Bull and the others, but not before he'd kissed my cheek. I smiled, knowing I'd handled myself right.

When we arrived at the table, Tank nudged his head toward me. "Beauty." He introduced everyone. "Bull, and his old lady, Letti. Styx and Lois. Bone and his old lady, Marie."

They all flicked their chins in greeting. Letti was dark-skinned like Bull, tattooed, and scowling at me.

Styx, who I knew to be Reaper's son, barely looked at me. The brunette on his lap got up and held out her hand. "Hey, sugar." I shook it. Bone and Marie were old. Like, really old. Marie looked haggard and worn, but her smile fucking lit up the room. As she pushed her aging body from her seat, I saw a small oxygen tank beside her. I smiled. She was rocking a cut with Bone's name on, and leather pants. "Fucking beautiful, honey."

"Thanks," I said and pointed to her pants. "Good taste." She winked and sat back down. Bull pointed at two seats beside him and Letti, and Tank and I sat down. Bull and Tank immediately started talking. Letti grabbed the bottle of whiskey and went to pour us two shots. She stopped and said to me, "Can you handle whiskey, or you more of a cooler girl?"

Her fucking sarcasm pissed me off. "Just pour the damn whiskey, darlin'. Whatever you pour I sure as shit can handle. Probably even drink your butch ass under the table."

"That so?" Letti said, and fuck if there wasn't a smirk pulling on her face. I knocked back the shot she poured then slammed the glass down and flicked my chin, telling her I wanted another.

After five shots, I asked, "Proved myself to you yet?" She was built for a woman, clearly lifted weights. She wore jeans and Bull's cut. Her eyes narrowed at me. I leaned forward. "Just 'cause I got big tits, a fucking spectacular ass, and the face of an angel doesn't mean I can't hang with you bitches, darlin'. Remember that."

Bull and Tank had stopped talking, and Bull was looking at his old lady like he was waiting for her to cast judgment on me. She finally shrugged and then poured me another. I knocked it back. "Most of the women here are sluts," she said. "Pining for Hangman cock to fill their rancid pussies. As long as you don't turn into one of them, we're good."

I pushed the empty shot glass to her. "Better stop fucking loading me with whiskey then, darlin'." My head swam. "Just checking . . . there's only one of you, right?" Letti's mouth dropped. I laughed. "I'm just fucking with you, darlin'. But all the same, cut me the fuck off from this wife-beating fuel and get me a wine cooler up in here!"

"I knew it," Letti said, but started laughing. My stomach squeezed at her smile, and the weight I'd been wearing on my chest since we entered here lessened some.

I wanted this for Tank.

I wanted this for us.

Lois stood up beside us as Styx got off his seat and pushed her off his lap. He was about to walk off when she pulled him back for a kiss. Styx pushed her away again after a second, then signed something to her. Lois's face fell slightly, and she watched him walk across the bar to Ky, who was all up in another woman who was looking at him with stars in her eyes.

Lois threw on her smile again and sat down. She took a shot then looked my way. "So, Beauty. Are you from Texas?"

I nodded. "Near Waco."

Lois nudged her head in Tank's direction. "You been together long?"

"'Bout six months now." I looked at Tank, who was talking to Bull and Bone.

Marie shuffled her chair closer. "There's been talk."

"What kind of talk?"

Marie inched closer still. Her voice was low and raspy, I guessed through years of smoking. She had an oxygen tube up her nose. When she lit up another smoke, I figured nothing was gonna stop her living her life. "'Bout your man. 'Bout making him a Hangmen prospect."

My heart started pounding. It was what he wanted. So damn much. "Who said that?"

Marie gave me a smug smile. "Pillow talk. Through the years Bone has got a little loose lipped." She laughed. "We're too old to give a fuck about Reaper's threats."

I laughed too.

"You want that?" Letti asked, eyes locked on me. I guessed she was trying to get a true read on my reaction.

I nodded. "Yeah. He's been lost. He needs a brotherhood to hold him down . . . as well as me."

"It's a hard life," Lois said as she looked across the bar at Styx.

"Are you his old lady?" She wasn't wearing a "Property of Styx" cut.

Lois whipped her head to me. All I saw was sadness on her face. "No . . . one day, maybe. When he finally wakes up and lets me in." She sighed. "I've known him his entire life. Loved him for as long as I can remember." She crossed her arms. Like it would protect her from something, some kind of inner pain. "But he's always loved someone else. Since he was a kid." She laughed, but there was no humor there. "Can't compete with a dream girl."

I had no fucking idea what she was talking about. Letti rolled her eyes like she was sick of hearing it, and Marie looked plain bored as fuck. But I couldn't help feel for the woman. I put my hand on hers and squeezed it for a second.

She squeezed it back.

"So what do you do?" Letti had poured more drink. I was gonna have to learn how to handle my liquor in this place.

I shook my head, wincing as the whiskey went down. I really wanted a fucking wine cooler. I wiped my mouth, careful of my red lipstick. "Waitressing now." I shrugged. "I was a pageant queen up until about six months ago." Letti raised an eyebrow. "Let's not talk about that," I said. Tank put his hand on my leg and I held his hand. "I always wanted to do retail," I said. "I love clothes. I mean, what bitch doesn't love shopping?"

"Me," Letti said.

"Okay, what bitch besides Letti doesn't love shopping?"

Marie nodded. "You good with numbers and shit?"

I shrugged. "I was good at math at school, I suppose. I like people. Love clothes." I smiled. "Especially if they're made of leather."

"I got a store," Marie said. "Sells biker shit. Lots of fuckin' leather." I stilled and stared at Marie. "I got a job if you want one." She pointed to her oxygen tank beside her. "I'm not as fit as I used to be and need a good sales girl."

"You serious?"

"As a heart attack."

"I'd love a job."

Marie lit up another smoke. "It's called Ride. It's not far from here. We sell biker shit, and also Hangmen merch for the hangers-on."

My gut squeezed as I realized she was serious. That she was offering me something I'd always wanted. Something I wanted to do, not something I was being forced to do, or *had* to do just to get by. "Thank you . . . I . . . I don't know what to say."

Marie pointed to Tank. "He'll hopefully be one of us soon. Which means you will be. Gotta keep all our businesses in the family."

Family. As fucked-up as this place was, I guessed it was one.

I hadn't realized Letti had got up until a bottle of wine was put down in front of me. "Might be shit. I found it in the back of the cellar. No fucking idea how old it is. No other asshole I know drinks that prissy shit."

"Thanks, darlin'," I said, truly touched.

"So, come on then, Beauty, tell us how you two met," Lois said, and I started the story. I held Tank's hand throughout. With every sentence spoken, I realized how lucky I was, and how much I loved the guy.

I'd never been so damn glad that I'd jumped on the back of his bike.

*****

One month later . . .

I shut the door of my truck behind me and ran my hand over the blue paint. Tank had bought it for me so I could get to and from work. I'd never owned my own truck before. She was my baby. I squinted up at the bright sun, then around the deserted compound.

Tank lifted his head from a bike as I approached the shop. My heart clenched when he stood, wearing nothing but his jeans and boots, oil smattered all over his abs and chest. Shit, he was ripped and huge and all fucking mine.

"Baby?" Tank said, confusion on his face. I lifted the Franklin's Barbeque bag so he could see. I looked behind him for Bull but couldn't see him. "Fuck. Yes," Tank said, taking the bag. He wrapped an arm around me. "You lined up all morning at Franklin's to bring me this?"

I hugged him back. "Sure did." I cast my eyes around the garage. "Where the hell is everyone? I bought enough to feed a friggin' small army."

Tank laughed as he put the barbeque down on the table. He hooked his arm around my waist. "They're all out on a run." I sighed when I saw the jealousy in his eyes. He wanted to be a prospect so fucking bad. But some of them still couldn't get over his Klan past. Marie had told me that certain members didn't trust that he wouldn't turn coat. Didn't trust he would protect the club against his old Klan buddies. Until they got a full house of yeses, Tank wouldn't ever be in. "They should be back soon."

Tank's head dropped. I stepped closer to him and ran my long red nails down his chest. "Then"—I slipped my leg between his, and my thigh grazed across his cock—"we have the place to ourselves?"

Tank smirked and pushed down the straps of my Ride tank. My bra strap came next. He had just pulled one cup down, exposing my right tit, when a loud smashing sound came from the shop's main entrance . . . at the gate. Tank lifted me out of the way and rushed to the front of the shop. He stilled, muscles bunching, then he spat, "Fuck!" He turned and pushed me to the back office. There was a door at the back that led to the Hangmen part of the compound. "Leave. Run!" Tank said, just as I heard a truck door opening.

My heart thudded in my chest. "Tank? What's happening?" My voice was shaking.

His eyes met mine. "Beauty, fucking run!" He went to turn away, but then pressed his mouth to mine and rasped, "I fucking love you, woman. Know that. I fucking love you." He shut the door to the office and turned the key. I tried the handle, but the fucker was locked. Pure fear lacing my veins, I ran to the window, hitting the glass, only to see three tatted-up skinheads walk toward Tank. My heart cracked, fucking splintered, then fell to the floor as I saw the looks on their faces . . .

. . . saw the guns and knives in their hands.

"Trace," Tank said. I was silent. Stock still as I listened through the glass.

"You fucking traitor. You motherfucking turncoat." The biggest of the three men—Trace—lifted a gun to Tank's face. I stopped breathing, was paralyzed as everything seemed to stop around me. Tank jumped forward, but the gun went off. Tank hit the floor, and I screamed a silent scream. Blood pooled under Tank, and the three Klan assholes started kicking him, punching him . . . killing him. I turned, not knowing what the hell to do. In panic, I punched through the exit door and out into the compound. I needed a gun. I needed something to help Tank.

I'd only taken a single step when I heard the deafening roar of motorcycles. Following the sound, a flicker of relief starting to build inside me, I sprinted to the front of the compound, heart thundering in my chest. Every rapid beat made me feel more and more sick.

The Hangmen were rolling in. "Help!' I screamed, my voice shaking. 'It's Tank! The Klan . . . they've found him . . . they're killing him!" My voice broke off just as Reaper, Big Poppa, and Bull all jumped off their bikes and a gunshot echoed around us, birds fleeing from the surrounding trees.

My heart fell. In that second I was sure I heard my soul scream out in agony.

"No . . . " I whispered.

Reaper pulled his Glock from his cut and smiled as he ran toward the bike shop. I ran too. I didn't give a shit if I wasn't supposed to. That was my man, the fucking love of my life, and I wasn't going anywhere.

As I rounded the corner, my feet stumbled at what I saw. Tank was on his feet, every inch of his bared flesh covered in blood. His right arm hung at his side, blood pouring from the gunshot wound and stab wounds that peppered his body. Two of the men were lying on the floor. One had a knife sticking out of his heart, and the other had a bullet in his forehead, his eyes open in death.

Trace was still in front of him. His gun was nowhere in sight, but his knife was in his hand and he was closing in on Tank. My baby was weak, his legs shaking and almost giving up on him. My hands covered my mouth as Trace lunged right at Tank's heart, but before Trace could get there, Reaper fired a shot straight into Trace's thigh. Trace fell to the floor. Tank looked up, eyes fucking blown and wild, until he saw the Hangmen closing in and me standing behind them. He seemed to take a long breath as he fell to the ground. I ran up to him, pushing past all the brothers in my way. I grabbed his hand. My vision blurred with tears.

Tank turned to Reaper. "Explosives . . . in the truck . . . were going to . . . blow . . . the club." My face paled. Reaper nodded, and a couple of the other guys dragged Trace away.

"Baby?" I whispered as Tank's eyes started closing. "He needs help!" I cried, inching closer to him and pressing my hand to the gunshot wound.

"Doc's on his way." Bull leaned down to press his hands to two of the biggest knife wounds. Leaning forward, I kissed Tank's lips, not giving one fuck if I got blood in my mouth. I kissed him and told him he was gonna be okay. He wasn't going anywhere without me.

I loved him. He had to survive.

I could no longer breathe without him.

CHAPTER FIVE

Tank

No fucking way. It couldn't be him.

Trace looked me dead in the eyes, and I saw the hatred, the fucking betrayal in his. "Trace." *I stood my ground.*

I knew this day would come. I knew that someone would have been pissed I was working for the Hangmen. I knew Tanner wouldn't have been able to keep them all off my back. My heart fucking fell when I wondered if Tanner knew about this . . .

"You fucking traitor. You motherfucking turncoat!" My hands fisted at my side as Trace lifted his gun and pointed it right at my face. The veins in his neck stood out as he shook with red-hot anger. He spat at my feet. "Turning from your white brothers for these impure cunts?"

"Yeah. I did." I saw the moment he made up his mind to shoot. I saw his snarl of pure disgust and just acted. Jumping forward, I knocked his hand enough to get it from my face, but the asshole managed to shoot and I felt the slug sink straight into my shoulder. I fell back from the force of the bullet, the fucking blistering pain slicing through me.

Trace and two other assholes I didn't even know let their boots fly, their fists. "No one fucking leaves the Klan alive," Trace spat as the back of his gun sliced across my face. He bent down and stared me right in the eyes. "You're gonna die, cunt. You're gonna die for turning your back and joining a club that lets in the impure—blacks and spics and motherfucking browns." I took a breath, glancing at one of the dicks to my side. His knife hung loosely in his hand as he rammed his boot into my side again and again.

I flexed my hand, then got ready. When he knelt down again, Trace's fucking mouth spurting shit I wasn't even hearing, I lurched, grabbing the guy's knife and stabbing him straight through his heart. The fucker fell above me, knocking his friend and Trace back. His mouth landed near my ear. He coughed and sputtered, his blood joining mine on my chest. So I shoved the knife deeper, twisting so the asshole would feel every single thing as the life drained from him.

Taking a long breath, I slid from under the asshole and got to my feet. His friend gave me no time to get my shit together. He flew at me, gun held out. But I'd been fighting for my fucking life since I was a kid whose pop wanted to use him as a punch bag. I'd taken out blacks and Mexicans and a whole bunch of Catholics and Jews under Landry. He'd made me his perfect solider. This asshole was nothing.

Slamming my elbow down on his arm, I grabbed the gun from his hand. I didn't even blink as I turned the gun on him and sent a bullet straight into his head. The asshole dropped, leaving me looking right at Trace. He was shaking with rage. "I fucking recruited you. Landry chose you over his soldiers who'd been with him longer, and you turned on us all, for what?"

"It's bullshit," I hissed out, blood and spit spraying from my mouth onto the ground. "It's all bullshit." I shook my head. "They just take in loser kids like us and fill our heads with bullshit."

"Traitor," Trace growled as he launched forward. He tried to grab me, but his hands slipped off my blood-soaked skin. His gun clattered to the ground, but when he came at me again, my strength faded and my gun slipped from my grip. Trace pulled a knife from the waistband of his jeans and launched himself at me. I stepped back, but it wasn't enough to completely get away from the blade. The steel sank into my side, and I heard a hiss of satisfaction slip from Trace's lips. The pain wasn't as great this time; my body was getting numb.

"You ain't gonna live," Trace said. I clamped my hand over my gunshot wound to stop the blood. My head was getting light

and my legs were giving way. Trace smiled. "Then I'm gonna blow this fucking place to the ground." He banged his free hand over his chest, right over his 88 tattoo. "No one fucks with the Klan. Landry will see who the true soldiers are in his army. The purest brothers. Then he'll let me in." My eyes ran to his truck. The explosives would be in there. We'd done it to a fuck-ton of impure businesses before. Torched their premises to the ground, preferably with them locked inside.

I had to stop him. Beauty's face popped into my mind. Her smile, her eyes, her fucking smart mouth. And I knew I had to stop him no matter what. The Hangmen liked her. I could see it. The old ladies loved her. They'd take her in. Look after her. Marie and Bone already thought of her as the daughter they never had.

I had to save my woman.

Trace tightened his grip on his knife. I reached into my pocket and grabbed the handle of the knife I'd taken from one of the pricks on the ground. Trace's foot rocked, ready to lunge, but just as he did, a shot rang out. He hit the ground. I took a breath, then my legs gave the fuck out . . .

"Baby?"

I tried to blink. My throat was a damn desert.

"Darlin'? Tank, baby?" Beauty's voice sailed into my ears and I felt her hands on my cheeks. I squeezed my eyes together before cracking them open, one at a time. Bright light scalded my eyeballs. I tried to move, but fire shot through my veins when I did.

"Fuck!" I hissed, my voice barely making a sound.

Beauty was there again. "Shh, baby. Careful." It took me a minute to open my eyes properly. A room with wood on the walls came into view. I looked down at my arm; a tube in it led to an IV beside me. I had bandages all over me and a brown blanket over my bottom half. Beauty sat on the bed beside me. I looked up and saw tears fall from her eyes and down her cheeks. Her hair, normally styled and big, was flat to her head. Not a scrap of makeup was on her face. She had one of my hoodies on—it fucking drowned her. She looked like a little lost kid.

"Baby . . ." I rasped, and she fell against me, wrapping her arms around me. I could feel her tears dripping down my neck. Fuck, my chest pulled apart at my woman breaking her heart. I lifted my arm, ignoring the sting from my right shoulder, and wrapped it around her head. I kept her the fuck close as she cried.

Then I realized the dream hadn't been a fucking dream at all . . . Trace . . . Trace had come after me and the Hangmen. I'd had to kill two of his men.

Beauty lifted her head. Taking hold of my face, she said, "I thought you'd died." She sniffed and wiped at her bare eyes. "I thought you'd left me." She hit me softly on my untouched shoulder, then dropped her head to mine. "Never fucking do that to me again. I don't care what happens—never lock me in a room where I can't get to you. Where I can't help."

"I wanted . . . you to be safe—"

"Fuck safe," she interrupted, her face tight and pinched. She meant every word. I couldn't help it. I smiled. Not just smiled—I fucking laughed. Beauty's mouth dropped open, and she hit me again, harder this time. "You're laughing?" But her lip twitched and then she was laughing too.

Grabbing her wrist, I pulled her to my chest, not giving one shit about the pain or the wounds that probably shouldn't have had my hundred-and-thirty pound woman lying over them. I made her look at me. "Fucking love you, woman."

"Love you too," she whispered back, and another tear fell. She laid her head on my chest, and I let her get rid of all the tears. I could hear people outside, and knew by the look of the room I had to be in the Hangmen compound. Well, by that and the massive Hangmen flag that covered the opposite wall.

"You killed two men." My eyes shot down to Beauty's blond head. She slowly lifted it so I could see her face. Her bottom lip shook. I nodded. Her eyes closed. "Just had to say it out loud."

"I've killed a fuck-ton more. You know it." I watched her for any kind of reaction. There was none. But she let out a long sigh. I pushed a piece of hair back from her cheek. "It's the life I live. I know you ain't seen it in the time we've been together." I looked around the room. At Hades' face looking down at me from the wall. Just like I'd ended up with the Klan, I had now found myself here. In a fucking den of killers.

I was a killer too.

Beauty looked away, but then turned her head to me. "I don't care." The weight that had been pressing on my chest as I waited for her reply lifted with those three words. She swallowed and moved in closer, until her lips hovered over my mouth. "I'm with you. No matter what. That's all there is to it." She smiled and stroked her finger down my cheek. "These past months with you have been the greatest of my life." She kissed my lips. "I'm not giving you up now. No matter what happens next."

Grabbing her head, I pressed my mouth to hers. Fucking tasting her and feeling that hot tongue against my own. I only pulled back when someone cleared their throat from the door. Over Beauty's shoulder I saw Bull in the doorway. Beauty didn't move away from me, just tucked her head into my neck and wrapped her arm around my waist.

"Good. You're awake," Bull said. He folded his arms over his chest, but his face looked different when he looked at me. More relaxed. I knew then that he'd always been somewhat guarded around me. But his eyes and jaw were less tense now. "Reaper wants to see you."

"He's just regained consciousness," Beauty argued, sitting up, Bull getting the brunt of her wrath. He didn't even flinch.

"It's okay." I threw the blanket off my legs and ripped the IV from my arm. "Jeans?" I asked Beauty.

"Tank—"

"Baby, I'm fine." Her eyes flared, but she got off the bed and disappeared into the hallway.

"She never fucking left your side," Bull said.

"How long was I out?"

"Couple of days. The doc we use kept you under the first day. You slept the rest on your own." I nodded, then Beauty came back into the room holding a bag from the store she worked at. She pulled out some jeans and helped me get them on. I could've done it myself, but I wasn't risking her cutting me the fuck down if I didn't let her help. She pulled out a shirt too.

"Don't need it." I held my injured shoulder as I got to my feet. Beauty helped me put on my boots. She backed away and folded her arms across her chest, looking down at the floor. I stopped in front of her and lifted her chin with my free hand. She kept her eyes cast down, until my patience won out and she met my eyes. "What?" she snapped.

"I'll be back soon. Then you can fuss over me as much as you fucking want, yeah?"

Beauty kicked the floor with her foot, looking too fucking adorable. But then she nodded, and a smile tugged on her mouth. She stepped closer until her chest was against mine. "Go." I kissed her on the mouth.

"Letti and Marie are in the bar waiting for you," Bull said. Beauty took my cell off the side table and put it in my pocket. "You need me, you call." Beauty wrapped her arms, in the too-long sleeves of my hoodie, around her waist, then hightailed it out of the room. I couldn't help but smirk. Fuck knows what she thought she could do against the Hangmen.

I followed Bull outside. It was early evening by the look of things. He led us to a big shed-looking structure away from the clubhouse. When he opened the door and we stepped inside, I saw all the Hangmen standing around the edges of the room . . . and in the center, tied to a chair, was Trace. His head lifted when I came in. My blood boiled to fucking lava in my veins as the cunt curled his fucking lip in disgust.

Suddenly, Reaper was in front of me. "Saved him for ya." He gritted his teeth, then relaxed. "Was fucking hard, but figure after this . . ." Reaper punched my bullet wound. Not hard, but hard enough to show me that he was fucking in charge. I breathed through the pain. "You should have the kill."

"Turncoat," Trace spat. I walked past Reaper and stood in front of the asshole who'd nearly taken me from Beauty. His face was beaten, his left eye almost closed. He smiled, and his teeth were washed with blood. "You deserve to die," he said, voice hoarse and raw. "You deserve to die on this fucking impure land." He roved his eye over the Hangmen. "This club used to be pure until they opened it up to the fucking inferior." He locked on Bull. "To black and brown scum that should be bowing at our superior feet."

Styx came up beside me and handed me a German blade. Fucking ironic for a Klansman to go out this way. I took the blade from his hand and faced Trace. "You think they won't keep coming for you?" Trace hissed. "Might not be now or soon, but one day the Klan will rise and take out the inferior races and those who left the brotherhood to fuck with the impure cunts below us."

I leaned forward and got right in his face. "That may be so. But just like you and the fucking sidekicks you dragged with you, I'll end them. Slit their fucking throats and piss on their dead corpses." Trace shook with rage. "The Klan don't mean shit anymore, just a bunch of dumbfuck assholes who hold on to the days of their granddaddies. The Klan will fall . . ." I smiled. "And if I have my way, I'll be leading the fucking charge."

Trace went to say something else, but I didn't give him chance to speak. I slashed my arm out and let Styx's German blade slice across Trace's throat. His open eye fixed on mine, and I watched him. Watched him choke on his own blood as the slit opened and poured crimson. I watched as he thrashed in the chair, fighting to breathe. And I watched as his eye frosted over and his body went still. There was no sound in the room except my breath. Then, with a fucking endless bellow from the pit of my stomach, I kicked his chair and rounded on his corpse as it crashed to the floor. I stabbed the cunt, stabbed and stabbed until there was nothing but blood and flesh. I stood and glared down on his carcass. I stepped back, breathless, to see the eyes of all the Hangmen on me.

I wiped the blade on my new jeans, but that didn't get it clean. I was covered in blood. I handed it back to Styx. The kid smiled. It was the first time I'd ever seen any expression from the mute Little Reaper.

"Now that was fucking awesome . . . I got a huge-ass boner. Anyone else?" Vike spoke, but I kept my eyes on Reaper.

"Church." Reaper turned to walk back toward the clubhouse. All the brothers left, and I was left looking down at Trace. Taking my cell from my jean pocket, I took a picture of Trace's fucked-up body and sent it to the one person I'd thought would never fucking betray me.

He didn't succeed. If you want me dead, fucking come get me yourself.

When the message sent, I walked from the shed, leaving the Klan firmly behind. I didn't go get Beauty; instead I took a shower in the room in which I'd been staying and threw the jeans away. I looked in the bag Beauty had brought in from Ride. Inside were another pair of jeans and a white shirt. I slipped them on, then sat down on the bed. I took a huge breath out. When I looked down, my hands were shaking. My legs couldn't keep still and adrenaline surged through my body, lighting me the fuck up.

Trace. Fucking Trace. The guy who took me off the streets and gave me a family. A family that were evil. I closed my eyes, thinking of that first night I'd helped them take out a rival gang member.

A black gang member . . .

Trace's loud laughter came from the driver's side as I sat beside him on the passenger seat. He turned the wheel, and I heard the sound of the body being dragged behind the car across Landry's land. Trace handed me the whiskey. Then he came to a stop. He got out of the car and I followed. We stopped at the back of the car. I looked down. And I didn't fucking move as I saw the state of the body.

"Another victory for the white race." Trace handed me a smoke. "Celebrate, Tank. You just got yourself your first kill . . ."

I pulled my hands down my face and felt my stomach fucking recoil at the memory. Because I'd been all in. Young, stupid, and high off my first kill, Trace fanning the flames of white pride.

Now, years later and grown the fuck up, I saw him for what he was . . . a fucking deadbeat loser who I'd put all my damn trust in. Followed the guy to hell with a burning cross lighting the way.

I was as stupid as his dead ass. Had innocent blood on my hands. Not all. Mostly rival gangs, but some that were just in the wrong place at the wrong fucking time.

I wasn't sure how long I'd been on the bed, but eventually I heard Bull's voice from the door. "You're needed in church."

I studied Bull's face, trying to work out what was going on. The guy's face was blank, not giving shit away. I followed, and as we made our way down the hallway, I let numbness fill me. Whatever was about to happen, good or bad, I wasn't getting away.

When I walked into the room that I hadn't ever been allowed in, all the brothers were sitting around a table. Reaper sat at the top, a gavel in front of him, Hades Hangmen patch on the wall behind him. Big Poppa was to his left, Styx to his right, Ky next to Styx.

The door shut behind me, but I kept my eyes on Reaper. If for some fucked-up reason he thought I'd brought the Klan here, I wanted to see the psycho coming at me. I wondered if this was some kind of test. Wondered if he'd kept Trace alive for me to see if I could do it. If I could kill a former Klan brother.

I tensed, fucking waiting for Reaper to speak, then he reached under the table and threw something at me. I caught it instinctively. The smell of fresh leather immediately shot to my nose. I glanced down to see a brand-new leather cut in my hands. It had the

Hangmen patch on the back. On the front was the word "Prospect", with my name beside it . . . Tank.

My head snapped up as my heart started to fucking slam in my chest. Reaper sat there in his chair like the fucker *was* Hades on his throne. A hand landed on my shoulder from behind. Bull.

"Well?" Ky said, smirking from his seat. "What the fuck you waiting for? Put it the fuck on."

Swallowing the lump in my throat, I slipped the cut over my shirt. And fuck, did it feel perfect. I ran my hand over the patch. "You fucking defended the Hangmen from your old brothers. Killed for us."

Reaper shrugged. "Showed you just might be one of us."

"I am," I said without taking a breath.

Reaper banged the gavel down on the table, the sound echoing off the walls. I heard that sound replaying in my head as I watched, in disbelief, the brothers get to their feet. I thought my heart was about to burst from my chest when I saw their faces, felt each slap on my back. My breathing was so hard I heard it in my own ears, the air rushing through me as fast as my blood rushed through my veins. Then I glanced down to my cut—*my fucking cut*—and read my name over and over again. "Tank" stitched into the leather . . . the smell of that leather telling me one fucking thing: I was a motherfucking Hangman.

I'm a motherfucking Hangman . . .

The world came crashing back into real time when Reaper came over, the last to reach me, Big Poppa beside him. "Prospecting is shit. Earn your dues, then one day you'll be patched in." I nodded, hanging off his every word. I was trying to take it in. Trying to believe it was true, that I wasn't still under from the attack and dreaming it all up in my head.

But I was here. As Reaper hit my shoulder in congratulations, I knew I was really fucking here. They'd let me in. Beauty and me . . . we were no longer on our own.

Bone came past me and took hold of my arm, dragging me toward the door of church. I frowned, trying to focus on what the hell was going on.

It was Big Poppa who spoke. "First you're getting those fucking Nazi tattoos covered. If I have to see them one more day I'll fucking slit your throat myself." Poppa clapped his hand down on my shoulder. "And my bike never ran so good. Don't wanna have to find a new mechanic." Bull and Ky pushed me into the bar. As the doors swung open, I immediately saw Beauty. Her blue eyes fell to the cut and the brothers standing around me, and her hands flew to her mouth.

My heart was a fucking iron fist when I saw the fucking happy tears sprout in her eyes, but I managed to smile. I didn't get a chance to go over because rock music came blasting through the speakers, a bottle of liquor was put in my hand, and I was shoved into a chair beside Bone, who emerged from the back room with his tattoo gun in his hand.

"Get the fuckin' sluts in!" Big Poppa called. "Time to get fuckin' wasted and fucked! We got a new brother!" My cut and shirt were removed and Bone started free-handing Hades cover-ups over my Nazi ink. And with every minute, I got more shitfaced, the tattoo gun erasing the final tie to my past life. The biggest fucking mistake I'd ever made.

As I looked up at Beauty, smiling and crying, drinking whiskey that I knew she fucking hated with Letti, Lois, and Marie, I felt like I could finally fucking breathe.

I was a motherfucking Hades Hangman.

And we were home.

EPILOGUE

One week later...

Beauty let loose a long fucking "Woohoo!" as we cruised down Congress Avenue, her arms in the air. Her vest, showing everyone who she belonged to, was on her back, tight black leathers on her long legs. She had her Hangmen tank on—Vike was right. It made her tits look unreal.

People stopped and stared as we went past. I rode and rode, until a familiar building came up ahead. The building I picked Beauty up from all those months ago. Beauty's arms came around my waist and her lips came to my ear, like she was reading my damn mind.

"Best fucking thing I've ever done, darlin'."

I smirked, knowing it was true. A fucking beauty queen in a crown and sash climbing onto my bike changed it all.

An hour later we were back in our home near the compound. The minute I got off the bike, Beauty jumped into my arms, legs around my waist—where they seemed permanently attached—and her lips on mine. Holding her ass in my hands, I carried her up the stairs to the porch, then through the front door.

We didn't get much farther, as when her hand reached into my jeans and she pulled out my already rock-hard cock, I lost my fucking mind.

Crashing her back against the wall, I quickly pulled down her leathers, pushing them far enough down her legs for her to toe them off. As always, my old lady wasn't wearing anything underneath. With how much we fucked, it didn't make sense to. I sunk three fingers into her already wet pussy. Beauty's head flew back and she moaned.

Her hand stroked at my cock. I pulled my fingers out and pushed her hand away, and in one long thrust, slammed my cock inside her. Her pussy clenched at my dick as I nailed into her, her back smacking against the wall. Beauty's red nails sliced into my back. She looked at me, eyes dazed and a smile on her face. Then she leaned in and bit my earlobe. "That what you call hard, darlin'? Fuck. Me. *Harder.*"

I groaned as I pinned her arms to the wall and let her fucking have it. Beauty's mouth dropped open and her moans grew louder. She always wanted it hard and fast after being on my bike. Since that was every day, my cock was barely out of her pussy. I sucked at her neck, hickeys bruising her skin. I fucking loved it. Showed the assholes coming into the shop and the compound that this woman was mine.

"Tank . . ." Beauty moaned, her pussy gripping me harder. "I'm coming . . ." I watched her face, watched her eyes close as her pussy squeezed my cock in a chokehold, her scream echoing around the room. That was all it took for my balls to tighten and for me to come too, filling her the fuck up.

My head fell against her neck. "You're gonna fuckin' kill me."

Beauty laughed and wrapped her arms around my neck. She pressed her lips hungrily to mine as I led us to the couch and laid us down, Beauty sprawling on my chest. "Mmm . . ." she murmured. "I love your big cock."

I laughed as she stroked it. "He likes you too."

Beauty smiled, but her eyes were closing. I held onto her as the sky turned dark outside. I carried her through to the bedroom and put her into bed. And I just watched her.

Best damn bitch here . . . I heard Ky's voice in my head, from last week at the clubhouse, as I was bitch-boy at the bar for the brothers. *She's born to be an old lady and live this life.* Styx and Ky had sat at the bar, watching with me as Beauty cleaned up the tables—all so my prospect ass wouldn't have to. I smiled at the memory, looking down as Beauty slept, blond hair spread all over the pillow. It had been Styx who'd signed it to me that day; Ky had translated it.

And it was true. Beauty had slipped straight into club life. Being a prospect was the fucking pits, but I knew what it led to. Kept my head down and did the bitch work like I was supposed to. Yet, if I was being honest, I knew I wasn't seen much like a prospect. Brothers didn't treat me like the others. More like one of them.

I looked down at the Hades tattoo on my hand, the final piece covered. Gone was the Nazi shit. Covered with images of my new family and club. New fucking brothers. Brothers I'd die for.

When I looked at Beauty, I knew I'd die for her too.

I was about to grab a shower when I heard a sound at the back door. Pulling my gun from the back of my jeans, I snuck through the house. A floorboard creaked again. I flicked off the safety, then flew into the kitchen, slamming on the light.

I pointed my gun, showing my fucking teeth as I realized who the fuck was standing in my house.

"What the fuck do you want?" Each of my words was thick with fucking poison. Betrayal and venom.

Tanner held up his arms. "I ain't armed, Tank." My eyes narrowed and I checked behind him. "It's just me. No one knows I'm here. I swear."

"Why?" I hissed, praying Beauty didn't wake up.

Tanner's face paled. Like he couldn't believe I'd asked the question. I thought I knew this guy. He was as close to me as a brother. "Why?" he echoed. "*Why?*" He shook his head, his eyes shining in the light. "Because I've been on tour for months, and I came back to fucking chaos at the ranch and my best friend sending me a picture of Trace's body and thinking I'd tried to fucking kill him. That's fucking why!"

"Trace came with two assholes I didn't even know and tried to kill me. Klan orders. Your bastard Klan!" I still had the bruises and cuts all over my fucking body. Tanner clearly saw them on my face too.

"It wasn't sanctioned," he said when I stepped closer, my aim at his head getting real fucking clear. "Landry never sent them. Last thing we need right now is a war with the Hangmen. I haven't been here. I don't keep much contact with the Klan while I'm away. It's too dangerous. I'm in the army, Tank. I can't be caught with Klan shit." I smelled bullshit in his answer. He must have seen it in my face. "Tank . . . I fucking swear it. Trace was losing favor with Landry and the Wizards. He was a fucking crackhead who Landry tossed aside months ago. He kept fucking up. Choosing snow over the brotherhood. He did this himself. He heard you were working for the Hangmen and planned the attack himself. He wanted back in." I thought of Trace, and his crazy fucking eyes as he waved his gun at me. He could have been high . . . I didn't fucking know. It all happened too quick.

Tanner's eyes fell to my cut and my new ink. His eyes widened, and I saw the anger build inside him. "You've joined them?" He shook his head, like he couldn't fucking believe it. "You serious? You're in the motherfucking Hangmen?"

Sighing, I lowered my gun. "I *am* a motherfucking Hangman. A prospect. I've left the Klan behind, Tann. I was serious when I walked away. I ain't coming back."

Tanner's face looked as though I'd fucking shot the gun and made a perfect hit. "I thought if you took some time away . . ."

"You thought I'd come back? To Landry?"

"We're your fucking family!" he hissed.

"Not anymore."

Tanner stepped back, wounded by my words. I could see the hurt in his eyes. He pulled out a chair and slumped down. I checked behind me for Beauty, but she must have still been asleep. Pulling out another chair, I grabbed two beers and put one in front of him. Tanner downed half the bottle before my ass had even hit my seat.

"What about me?" he croaked, then lifted his eyes. "I'm your brother. Your fucking best friend." His forehead creased in confusion, then he asked, "If we're no longer your family, who the fuck am I to you now? Your enemy? We were meant to lead the Klan into the new age. Me as the leader, you by my fucking side. We had plans, Tank. Big fucking plans."

My chest cracked at the hurt in his voice. White power or not, White Prince of the fucking KKK or not, Tanner Ayers *was* my fucking brother. We'd grown from boys to men together. Fuck, he was still young. Lethal, but young. "Thought you'd sent them. Thought you'd fucking ordered the soldiers to take me out."

"Then you don't know me at all." Tanner's eyes were steel.

"I do. That's why I thought it was true." The fucker was ruthless. Killed without thought. The brother killed like he had no fucking heart. I had too . . . but he was on another level. Best Klan member they'd ever had. Raised with it. Tanner Ayers *was* the Ku Klux Klan. The two went hand in hand.

His lip curved. "Not you. You might be the only person on this planet I'd never kill." He sipped his beer and ran his hand down his face. "I tracked you down to this house. It wasn't hard." He flicked his chin in the direction of the bedroom. "Saw you got yourself a woman now." He smirked. "Clearly still have Aryan tastes even though you can't bear to be around us."

I ignored the last part. "I'm not trying to disappear, to live in secret. I'm here. I'm with the Hangmen. No point in fucking hiding. We share the same city. Live in the same fucked-up world away from the 'normal' people."

"Tank, you're white power. One of the fucking elite!" He pointed at me. "That's who you are inside. Who made you. We bleed the fucking same red, white, and blue, pure WASP blood. You can't just turn your back on us for the motherfucking Hangmen!" He laughed, no humor. "You think we're bad? Do you know who you're in with now? The Hangmen? They kill worse than we ever do. Reaper Nash murders for fucking fun, but *we're* the wrong ones? Your family, who has a real cause, a real fucking war we're gearing up for? You think the Hangmen are a better for fit you?" His lip curled in disgust. "You think I don't know you've been hanging with a Samoan? Really, Tank?"

I let the comment about Bull go. Tanner would never understand how I could befriend him. He gave no one outside the white race his time. "I don't bleed the white and red no more. My blood is as fucking black as Hades now, brother." I paused. "We're no longer the same."

The room was thick with tension. Tanner's face lost any expression, and I knew I was now sitting with Tanner Ayers, the cold Klan bastard his daddy had groomed him into. The White Prince who thought of nothing or no one outside the Klan.

"I should kill you." The hairs on the back of my neck stood on end at the threat and the tone of Tann's deep voice. But that went away. Because despite the way he was looking at me now, he was right. He wouldn't touch me.

And there was no more to be said between us.

Tanner glared at me, and I could see the war he was fighting in his mind in his narrowed eyes. "You know too much . . . about me, about my old man . . ." Tense minutes followed.

Suddenly, Tanner finished his beer and got to his feet. He walked to the door. "Some shit's going down at the brotherhood. I need to be there. I gotta go."

My first instinct was to ask what was happening. To tell him I had his back, that we'd figure it out together . . . but I no longer did. And that part of all this clusterfuck of a situation was what hurt the most.

"We done?" I asked, my voice cutting out near the end of the question. Not done right now. Not done with this conversation. Tanner knew I meant in life. The end of our friendship. Were *we* done for good.

Tanner's head dropped forward. He put his hand in his pocket. A burner cell came flying straight at me. "Seems fucking not."

"You'll be in charge one day," I said. He got what I was really saying. There'd come a day when the brotherhoods we belonged to would matter.

Tanner's shoulders tensed. "Yeah. And the Klan'll be the greatest fucking power in the States. I'll make fucking sure of it." I sighed. He *had* to know that all the Klan ideology was bullshit. But Tanner had been raised in Klan life. He *was* white power. And I knew when he was in charge, he *would* make them the greatest power.

Fuck knew what we'd do then.

Tanner turned the doorknob.

"You'll realize it one day, Tann. Something will happen one day to make you forget all this white power shit. That all the 'color making us different' crap isn't real. You'll know one day that you need to walk the fuck away."

Tann stayed silent on those fucking words, but then said, "You know where I am if you need me." Then he was out the door. I heard his Fat Boy pull away down the street.

I sat on my chair for a fucking age, staring at the bottle of beer and the cell. I knew I should destroy it. Cut all ties. Or I should keep it, tell the club and use Tanner for intel. Use him to protect the Hangmen. But when I got to my feet and walked to the safe, locking the cell away, I knew I couldn't and wouldn't do that. Though that would be my secret. Reaper would kill me stone dead if he knew I was best friends with the future White Prince.

I locked the doors, stripped off my clothes, and got the fuck in bed with my bitch. I slipped off her tank and bra as she slept, then pulled her to my chest. Tanner had to come around one day. Because one day the Hangmen would go to war with the Klan. War always came around in this life. And when that day came, I didn't wanna face the best friend I'd ever had. Didn't wanna choose between him and the club.

I had no idea what the hell I'd do.

"You okay, darlin'?" Beauty's sleepy voice cut through my thoughts. Her hands trailed over my chest, like she could sense I was all fucked up inside.

"Mm . . ." she murmured, then started kissing my abs. Lifting her up, I brought her lips to my mouth.

As I took her tongue, I pushed all thoughts of Tanner aside. It was up to my brother to find his way from that life. Something would happen one day to make him question it all. He was too smart for it not to.

As Beauty broke from my mouth and kissed along my chest, I knew, despite what Tanner said, I'd fucking hit the jackpot. I had a club I loved, a brotherhood that fit. I worked on bikes all day . . . but best yet, I had this fucking woman by my side. Through all the shit that had come our way, she stood strong. A fucking rock, a damn diamond by my side. In my bed and on the back of my bike.

I flipped Beauty onto her back. "Love you," I said, making sure she was looking into my eyes when I said it.

"I love you too," she whispered back, tears in her eyes. She stroked her hand down my cheek. "I love you so much, darlin'."

I kissed her, then I pushed my hand between her legs. "You ready for me?"

"Always, Tank," she whispered. "Always."

THE END

PLAYLIST

My Arms Were Always Around You — Peter Bradley Adams

Lost It All — Jill Andrews

The Place I left Behind — The Deep Dark Woods

Don't Know Who I Am — Rebecca Roubion

When You Break — Bear's Den

I Know What I Am — Band Of Skulls

Run —Leona Lewis

One Day Like This — Elbow

Forever By Your Side (with JOHNNYSWIM) — NEEDTOBREATHE

Passion — HIGHSOCIETY

Wild Love — James Bay

Hell Or High Water — Passenger

Best Days — Lissie

Such A Simple Thing — Ray LaMontagne

ACKNOWLEDGEMENTS

Thank you to my husband, Stephen, for always being my rock..

Roman, I never thought it was possible to love somebody so much. You're the best thing I have ever done in my life. Love you to bits, my little dude!

Mam and Dad, thank you for the continued support.

Samantha, Marc, Taylor, Isaac, Archie, and Elias, love you all.

Thessa, thank you for being the best assistant in the world. You make the best edits, keep me organized and are one kick ass friend to boot!

Liz, thank you for being my super-agent and friend.

To my fabulous editor, Kia. I couldn't have done it without you.

Neda and Ardent Prose, I am so happy that I jumped on board with you guys. You've made my life infinitely more organized. You kick PR ass!

To my Hangmen Harem, I couldn't ask for better book friends. Thank you for all for everything you do for me. Here's to another step forward in our Dark Romance

Revolution! *Viva Dark Romance!*

Jenny and Gitte, you know how I feel about you two ladies. Love you to bits! I truly value everything you've done for me over the years, and continue to do!

Thank you to all the AMAZING bloggers that have supported my career from the start, and the ones who help share my work and shout about it from the rooftops.

And lastly, thank you to the readers. Without you none of this would be possible. Our Hades Hangmen world is one of my very favorite places to be. Some people don't understand us, and our undying love for our favorite men in leather… But we have each other, our own tribe, and that's all we'll ever need as our biker series grows!

Our Hangmen world kick ass!

"Live Free. Ride Free. Die Free!"

AUTHOR BIOGRAPHY

Tillie Cole hails from a small town in the North-East of England. She grew up on a farm with her English mother, Scottish father and older sister and a multitude of rescue animals. As soon as she could, Tillie left her rural roots for the bright lights of the big city.

After graduating from Newcastle University with a BA Hons in Religious Studies, Tillie followed her Professional Rugby player husband around the world for a decade, becoming a teacher in between and thoroughly enjoyed teaching High School students Social Studies before putting pen to paper, and finishing her first novel.

After several years living in Italy, Canada and the USA, Tillie has now settled back in her hometown in England, with her husband and new son.

Tillie is both an independent and traditionally published author, and writes many genres including: Contemporary Romance, Dark Romance, Young Adult and New Adult novels.

When she is not writing, Tillie enjoys nothing more than spending time with her little family, curling up on her couch watching movies, drinking far too much coffee, and convincing herself that she really doesn't need that last square of chocolate.

FOLLOW TILLIE AT

https://www.facebook.com/tilliecoleauthor

https://www.facebook.com/groups/tilliecolestreetteam

https://twitter.com/tillie_cole

Instagram: @authortilliecole

Or drop me an email at: authortilliecole@gmail.com

Or check out my website:
www.tilliecole.com

For all news on upcoming releases and exclusive giveaways join Tillie's newsletter. http://eepurl.com/bDFq5H

Subscribe to Tillie's YouTube channel: 'Tillie Cole'

Made in the USA
San Bernardino, CA
07 December 2018